Dear Jane,

May you enjo

as much as I enjoyed writing
it!

Sidewinder
Precision Pro

All the best

Douglas Porter

First published for Amazon Kindle 2016

This edition 2016

Copyright © 2016 Douglas Porter

All rights reserved.

ISBN: 1534833781
ISBN-13: 9781534833784

DEDICATION

As all authors with wives and families must do, I gladly dedicate the book you are about to read to my wife Judith and our sons William and George.

However, as you will see when you reach the end of the story, there are a few others I need to thank as well. First things first, though.

SIDEWINDER PRECISION PRO

They don't pay enough for this job.

'Course, when I took the job, it was more money than I'd ever seen in my life. Enough to save some, maybe dream of retiring on some planet somewhere that has good housing, enough government to keep the bandits off of the farm your family spent three generations trying to build up, maybe some luxuries and good doctoring, and meanwhile there's enough to spend at the end of a hitch on some fun times with a girl, or maybe a boy if that's what you prefer. It ain't to my taste, much, but I guess if I think of settling down some time –

But that's all by the by. I'm not saying I'm the best there is at what I do, but up to now it's been good enough to bring me back. 'Course, anyone else in this business can say the same – 'cos anyone who can't say it, well, they ain't in the business any more and they ain't saying much of anything to anyone either. That's the kind of crack we fling around when we're in the station and we got a night-cycle to kill and we're still too wired to sleep, which is how it goes down most times once we dock.

Some runs are just straight out, through the wormhole

and in again, when you figure either the goonies haven't got the word that there's a fat trader coming through or else GalCop's doing its job better than usual, or even that we've earned our pay the best way of all by scaring off anyone that might have been looking to score some free cargo. Mostly it's not that way, though.

That's when it gets to be real lonely out there in a singleship with no Witchdrive, likely in a system that's got no time for your kind if it happens that your mothership goes down and you've got no-one left to make you a wormhole, and all you have to keep yourself alive is a front laser, some energy banks, and a ship you sure hope can turn tighter than what it can't outrun. That, and some hullmetal, a water spigot and a couple of tubes of peanut paste, plus a pair of spaceman's pants – the kind you won't be washing and using again – is your own little universe for a few hours, plus some more thinking-it-over time in Witchspace assuming you and your wingmate didn't bump each other trying to get in the wormhole at the same time.

Still, like I say, up to now I'm shooting straighter and ducking faster than the enemy, and that's good enough for one day at a time, which is mostly how we live. There's a kind of group spirit, for sure, but we don't make what you'd call real close bonds.

Although –

There was this time in Tionisla Station, when we'd just got in from Isinor and riding guard on a rustbucket of a Python. We'd gotten bounced by another Python and his buddies out near the Witchpoint (and listen to me talking like an old spaceman. You'll laugh when I tell you about my homeworld), and for once everything went right and we even scored some bonus money from the salvage to go with not losing so much as one of us, and you bet that was a night to party.

Well, Conor and I were laughing away, each of us with one arm round a girl, and mine was pouring a stream of Blue Fire straight out of the spout into my mouth while Conor's was doing the same for him, and he meets my eye and says "Want to make up a foursome? My room's plenty big enough," and I thought it over and said "Why not? But we're not touching each other!" and laughed.

Anyhow, the girls went along with it – and believe me, in the spacers' bar, not the fancy one for the rich traders and playboys but the one they keep for the real fighting pilots, and you'd better believe you're in for a fight if you try to come in when you hadn't oughta, you get all sorts, and they aren't even there to make any money, they're just there for the crazy fun – and if Conor was disappointed he didn't do more than look it for a moment. Maybe he just wanted to watch and compare. I figured I could live with that.

For my money Conor had scored a little medical aid, which was something else I'd never heard of until I saw my first Coriolis station, but then, he had to keep up with me – and he was doing it, too. The girls found it interesting enough to compare notes and then swap over, and I don't reckon either of them went away disappointed when the dawnside crescent showed through the porthole.

Before then though, while it was still dark and we'd caught some sleep in an every-which-way tangle of arms and legs, I got one of the girls to move over and let me take her place, and I had a go at waking up Conor in a nice way while it was still black dark. If he knew who it was he didn't let on, and I figure I didn't do it badly at that, though I don't want to change over from girls for realsies.

We were all back in our own places, allowing for the tangle I just mentioned, before it got light enough to see, and next morning it was business as usual – which this time meant I stayed with the rustbucket and Conor signed up along with a rich man in a Fer-de-lance that was going another way, and who knows whether we'll be meeting again soon, late or ever? That's why we don't make real close bonds.

So for now it's just me and my Sidewinder, shooting what I'm paid to shoot, and trying to make sure someone doesn't do unto me first.

* * *

It turns out that Qudira has some rich neighbours with a lot of technology.

Not that I knew anything about this when I was growing up. I didn't look up at the night sky all that often, and even then, only when the skies were a lot clearer than usual. I grew up thinking everywhere had loads of volcanoes – No, that's not true. I grew up thinking our volcano-studded, sulphurous, cloudy, damp, backward little planet was everything there was in the universe. There was Down Here, and there was Lights in the Sky, and the only place anything lived was Down Here.

One or two of the smart kids at school – if you'd call it school. Most of us could just about read and write, and there wasn't much to read or to write with, except now and then when one of those mystery boxes turned up and we had some lessons for a few weeks if there was nothing else that we needed to do – anyway, one or two of the smart kids at school reckoned there were people Up There too. Where I lived, there was a little moon that was always low down near the ground line, about where the sun set in the middle of winter. It didn't always shine, but when it did, it was always in the one place – and it was small next to the real moon, but it was way bigger and brighter than a star. The smart kids said there were men in the little moon, and sometimes they came down to visit, and that was why the mystery boxes turned up now and then and why Grandpa could always sell the "water" he made in his shed to Trader Jho.

These days I hardly know where Qudira is any more. It's a hard place to pine for, even when the laser beams are glittering in the dust or the attack ships are on fire off the shoulder of Begeabi. Space is big and cold, but when all's said and done the warmth of a home doesn't mean anything when the hearth's been ground to dust underfoot and the last home fire you saw was the one you wanted to put out but couldn't.

Once it was all gone and the screaming had stopped,

and I'd waited until everyone left and gave them until after sunset before I came out of the hollow tree and picked through all the ashes, and it finally sank in that everything was burnt down and destroyed, I set myself for a long walk.

The way I saw it was like this. If there was anyone up there in the little moon, and if they ever came down, there must be – Well, I didn't know how anyone could get down out of the sky, but I figured, where they would come down would be right under the little moon, so all I had to do to meet myself a moon man was to walk until the moon was overhead, and since it never moved, sooner or later I could do that. You need to remember I'd never even seen a map, and I didn't know where anyone lived once I was half a day's walk from home.

Anyway, I'd not been on my way long when I fell in with an old-timer. He wasn't in a much better way than I was, and I figure now he was just going home to die, but he was glad of a young pair of legs to step and fetch for him a few days, and I helped him out for a week or two. After a bit I kind of trusted him enough to tell him where I was going, and he laughed, but not unkindly.

"That's further'n I ever went," he said, "or'll be goin' now, but there may well be men up in Coriolis – that's what they call her, so they tell me. An' you wants to be careful if'n you're goin' that way. I hear where they take kids like you up there, an' no-one ever sees 'em again – still, you'll be knowin' your own business best."

It was just getting dark, with the little moon still hanging there in the sky, and he reached into his pack and brought out something I'd never seen before – something made of iron and weighing a couple of pounds, with a little bit of glass in each end, and you could look through it, both eyes at once. He showed me how they worked and got me to try out looking at some things nearby – trees and bushes to begin with, then a smoker up on one of the slopes. Then he said "Now try lookin' at Coriolis through her."

I did like he said, and I had to hold the thing mighty

steady to stop that little circle of white jumping about all over the place, but eventually I got it done, and he said "If'n you got her clear in your sight, you watch real close for a minute or so," and I once again did like he said. For a little while I couldn't see what he might be driving at, then I put them down and gasped and looked at him.

"It's spinning around," I said.

"Yup," he chuckled. "Ain't that something, though? Ain't nothing else up there that does that."

It was a clear night for once, with lots of stars out and the moon coming up for the second rising, and I looked at everything I could through that thing, especially the moon, which was about the most beautiful thing I ever saw. Nothing else was spinning like Coriolis did, though, which carried on right the way it was going until it disappeared a few hours after dark.

That night I cuddled up closer to the old-timer than before, and we fell asleep like that by the fire, him snoring and smelling funny, and Coriolis kept on spinning in my head.

* * *

No-one lives for ever.

The old-timer told me that before I moved on, and I guess I already knew that pretty well just from how I'd been raised, but it's plenty true when you fly a singleship for a living. Most times when I fly out with a freighter and a bunch of other hired guns, there's someone doesn't make it, either one of us or one of the guys that try to stick up our freighter. The pay's already banked, of course, and those of us that have next of kin mostly make arrangements ahead of time to have it forwarded if we don't make it back, but some of us don't, and unless we're feeling charitable and have remembered that this might be the mission we don't come back from and so decide ahead of time which stranger ought to get it, I guess sooner or later it makes its way back to the government or our employer.

Once I'd seen Coriolis through that viewing-thing, I was keener than ever to get to it, and the old-timer seemed to know it. He out and said it himself one day: "Time to move on, kid, if you're ever to meet your man in the moon". Winter wasn't so far off by then, but one way and another it was likely I'd be travelling through at least one winter before I got where I was going, and I figured I could probably manage.

We had one last sit by the fire, then he dug through his pack one more time and fetched out something else which I'd never touched before, though this time I knew what it was and what it was for. He still spelled everything out for me though, before he even let me touch it. "This is for making people be dead," he said. "Whatever else you might do with it, that's what it's for. You don't ever point this end at anyone you want to still be alive when you're through, and if you ever do point it at someone, you finish what you started as quick and sure as you can."

It seemed to fit my hand like it'd been made for it, and he showed me how to load it and which bit to press to make it fire. Then he said "Keep it where you can get at it, and make sure you know how to use it and be sure you can hit what you point it at. I ain't got many loads for it and I never met a man who knew how to make 'em, but there's some that will have some for sale if you ask around careful-like. Mebbe the moon-men bring them."

I laughed at that, like he meant me to, but it turned out he was dead right as far as that went.

Well, before I moved on I practised a little bit, just to be sure I knew how to use it, and I found it pretty easy to hit what I pointed it at, and even from a standing start with the piece down the waistband of my pants I could fetch it out and hit my mark pretty quick. At the time I didn't much want to use it to put a hole in a living human being, but when I thought back to how my home burned down – which wasn't something I thought about very often – I decided there might be worse things that could happen, at that.

"This is quite the present you're giving me," I said, "and I ain't rightly got anything I can give you back for it."

He laughed hisself. "Kid, if you was six month older and I was even a couple of years younger, I'd have a suggestion for you. But I figure it's a mite too early for you an' I know for a cold fact it's way too late for me. Keep it an' use it in good health – only make sure you really do need someone dead before you use it on 'em. Once they're gone, there's no second thoughts and no bringin' back."

That's a thought that's stayed with me ever since, but there's a time and a place to think it, I've found. When you're in the cockpit and there's the stink of fear all around you – and you're way better than me if you keep your pants dry all through the part where your laser's hot and your energy running low, and there's still more of the other side than you, and your wingmate's gone in a burst of fire and all you can do is hope it didn't hurt – that's not the time to be asking yourself "You know, does this person need, real-bad need, to be dead right now?". Nope. If you want to live through to the next fun time with a bottle, a girl and maybe a colleague or two that has the same idea as you, you just concentrate on keeping out of someone's sights and getting your own locked on for long enough to let them have it.

After my old friend and benefactor, I kept myself pretty much to myself through the months that followed, barring an overnight with someone else who might be headed the same way and have a use for some company on the road, and I was just as glad that I didn't have to use my gun very often. Every few days Coriolis looked a little higher in the sky, as the winter wore away into spring and I had to score myself some new boots 'cos I'd worn the old ones out.

Then one night (but I'd not kept up my count) I saw something dropping from the sky on a pillar of blue fire, like it was going to hit just beyond the hills, and after the next sunrise but one – well, I never knew there could be so many buildings all together in the one place.

* * *

14

I'd been in the spaceport for about half a day before I had to shoot anyone.

Actually "spaceport" isn't quite it. On Qudira at least – it may be different in other places – there's the ground station itself, which has GalCop money behind it and a bundle of extra cash on account of all of the trade coming through, and all of this allows for a lot of building with, at the very least, piped water and sanitation and switched power and a whole lot else, and the buildings are up to code and don't fall down for anything short of an asteroid strike. I stood there on the hillside just watching it in the distance for I don't know how long; we didn't really count in hours when I was young – you got up with the sun, worked, ate, worked some more, took a break at noontime in the hot season, worked some more, came home when the sun was nearly down, ate and then went to bed – but it couldn't have been a whole morning at any rate. Not only was it bigger than I'd ever believed possible but it was whiter, too.

And then there was the part outside the station walls, which was still bigger than any settlement I'd seen, imagined or heard tell of. I'd come from very far away, but plenty of folks that lived closer and had heard of the station had left their old life behind and come to see what the spacer city looked like. And it was a sight to see, too: Coriolis was right overhead, but I'd never felt less like looking at it than I did right then. Unfortunately, thousands of folks had come all this way to look for a better life, and thousands of them found out that thousands more had got there first.

So you had this sprawl outside the station that went on for what seemed like a half-day's walk, clustered around the river so they had somewhere to get water from, and there were too many folks crowded in too close with no proper way to earn a living. Some of them had day jobs in the station, but they couldn't afford to live there on what they got paid; some of them maybe had the money, but they weren't the sort that GalCop law wanted about the place; most of them seemed to make a living off each other, don't ask me how.

I wanted a closer look at the station, but it was pretty clear that I was already shooting for the moon in trying to get myself a place at the shanty town, which stank worse than any farmyard I'd ever seen and was a sight unhealthier besides. I mean, in all my life I'd never seen a place where kids played with sewage running in the open all around them, nor even heard of people trying to earn a crust scavenging trash off city dumps. We had a market town a day's journey from home that we went to maybe twice a year, but even that didn't have a big pit set aside for people to throw trash in.

Mind you, the spaceport trash included a few things that would have passed for wealth back at home, where if you could burn it, build with it or even keep the rain off with it then it wasn't trash in the first place.

Anyway, by the time it was getting towards sunset, I was mighty hungry and there wasn't much to be done about it, and perhaps that's what made Fat Hannah notice me – though I didn't learn her name till later. I was walking by a kind of a stall built on the front of a shack, and there was a cooking smell and I stopped to sniff at it, and this huge woman asked me was I hungry, and there was no sense lying about it.

"You poor kid," she said, kind of motherly except neither my mother nor anyone else I'd ever seen could afford to eat enough to flesh up like that. "Just get in, did you? Come and have yourself a bite to eat."

There was a covered area behind the stall where a bunch of people were all tucking in, and if there was anything the matter with it, nobody was complaining. Fat Hannah put a bowl of stew and a spoon in front of me and watched me put the grub away, and served up another ladle-full when the first was gone. Then she said, with a wink, "You know, you look grown-up enough for a little something to help that go down. The first one's on the house." And she popped her hand in her apron and came out with a little bottle of what looked like sugar candy – the kind we only saw on market days. She held one out to me.

"You want to be careful about that, child," said a thin-faced man I'd not noticed before. He wasn't eating – just looking around the entrance to the eating area. "This could go two ways. Either you'll feel real good, and then you'll want some more, and before two days have gone you'll be ready to do anything to get just one more, and I mean anything no matter what your momma told you never to do… or you'll wake up somewhere with a strange sky and a strange face looking at you, and be in for all sorts of adventures where you'll never be coming home again."

Fat Hannah screamed in rage and yanked a gun out from under her apron, and then there was a bang, and she was stood there looking at where the gun wasn't in her hand any more, and I was looking too, and trying to decide whether that was really what I'd meant to do just then, because it wasn't quite how the old-timer had said things ought to go when you pull a gun.

* * *

You got to know when to walk away, and know when to run.

When you're on escort duty, you can only run away so far. It's no good to anyone if your freighter buys it – you can pretty much kiss goodbye to your chances of an honest job in future if you let that happen, unless the record shows real clear that you were doing your darnedest to stop it. Also, when your wingmates catch up to you next, the least you can expect is to be kicked black and blue for running out on them, and maybe getting tarred and feathered and rolled around the docking bay in a barrel so everyone knows what you did. It hardly ever happens because it hardly ever needs to.

But everyone understands if you need to shake a little heat and get someone to pull a bogey off your back. That's one thing we're all glad to do for one another, 'cos we know it's a matter of when not if we're going to need the same favour ourselves. And sometimes a trading convoy and a pirate rig will turn up in-system at the same time, and it turns out both sides know how to count after all, and you'll get both teams sidling away from each other and, as it were, making sure they're not the first to blink, or else a furball will be starting up and it won't end while either side's got one ship left able to shoot.

After I'd shot the gun out of Fat Hannah's hand, and long before I'd decided whether I'd done it on purpose, there was dead quiet in the little eatery. The thin-faced man was the first to speak.

"Nobody move," he said. "You've got a gun here in the hands of a scared kid that knows how to use it, and that's how people get shot with nobody meaning it. Kid, ease your way over here nice and slow, and don't point that thing at anyone unless they try to grab you. Don't stand where I can reach you when you get here. The rest of you, don't commit suicide."

Everyone sat right where they were. Even Fat Hannah kept quiet, though she was wringing her hand like she had a sprain, while I did what the thin-faced man said. I stopped out of his reach and I saw why he'd said so – so I wouldn't think I had to shoot him to be safe. He backed off into the street, if that's not a word that's too fancy for an open sewer, and I edged after him.

"I'm carrying too," he called out. "Anyone who doesn't show their face out here won't have anything to worry about." And then to me, a lot quieter, "Nor will we, if we don't shoot anyone. Once we start, we'd need to shoot more than you or I have got loads for. So we ease our way out of here and bank on no-one being in a hurry to die."

There was a cab – another word I had to pick up later – fifty metres up the alley, and the thin-faced man opened the door, beckoned me inside, then came in after me and snapped "Station-side. Sector office." It didn't mean a thing to me, but the cab lurched into movement without a moment's delay, and if any of Fat Hannah's neighbours planned on making something of it for her, we didn't get to find out.

You can't believe how different Station-side looked, sounded and smelled once you'd been in the shanty-town. The thin-faced man watched me and grinned at my expression. I didn't mind one bit. Everything was so bright and clean, and so much light that I'd never seen anything like after sunset. If I had my mouth wide open everywhere we went, well, I had reason. By now I had the weapon on safety and put away again, which made us both a lot less tense.

"Agent Elus," said the thin-faced man, "Galactic Cooperative Light Escort recruiting officer for the Northeast Octant, GalSector 1... and you haven't the faintest idea what I just said, have you?"

His grin was infectious and I answered it with a similar one, or so I hoped. "No. Except the first bit was your name? Are you from Coriolis?"

"I came through the Coriolis Station on my way down – there isn't any other way to get here," Elus said, "but I'm from Aate, a little less than seven light-years over. But... you know what, let's begin at the beginning, and not tonight.

"First off, did you mean to shoot that gun out of Fat Hannah's hand or was that a pure fluke?"

"I'm not sure," I said. "But maybe I didn't want to shoot her. She'd just fed me – and you shouldn't shoot women."

"That's what a lot of people think, all over the Eight," said Elus. He opened the cab door and showed something to the driver, and ushered me out. "My office. But anyway, be warned, not everyone thinks so – and also, you can't always tell whether you're shooting at a woman or a man anyway."

"Well, anyway, I didn't want her to shoot you either, because if you were telling the truth then you were doing me a favour, and even if you were lying, you shouldn't shoot someone just for telling lies," I pointed out.

"I kind of wish it was lies, but unfortunately, Fat Hannah's guilty of everything I said. But we've got enough to pin on her now – 'we' meaning the police, not me, but we help each other. Still and all, I'm not sorry how things went down. I'll tell you why. I'm guessing you made your way here to look for a job, maybe even get off this sad little apology for a colony world. And in that case, consider yourself talent-spotted – because it's not every girl I meet that can shoot as fast and as straight as you."

* * *

The thing with being ignorant is you don't realize how ignorant you are.

See, nowadays there's a load of stuff I figure I'll always be ignorant about, but I know enough to know what I don't know, if that makes sense. Like, up in the snout of my Sidewinder there's a laser, and I can talk fancy as you like about "coherent light", but I know that deep down I don't understand how there can be such a thing as a light that's bright enough to burn holes in solid metal and it might as well be magic for all I can explain it. Same story with my ship's drive, I can't tell you why it is it'll keep running practically for ever, and however much I read up on the theory I don't come away any the wiser. But I know how to shoot things with a laser and I know how to use the drive to make my ship go faster and slower, and at least I can say "It's a machine. I don't know how it works, but I know someone who knows how to make 'em and how to fix 'em, an' if I studied hard enough an' learned stuff in the right order I'd be able to do that too."

The day I took my first cab ride, I barely even grasped there was such a thing as a box on wheels you could get in and ride around in, though it was a little bit like a farm cart so far as that went. I figured "Agent Elus" was a man's name, but I found out a while later that "Agent" was what he did, not who he was, same as "Coriolis" was a word for a kind of a thing up above the sky, not the name of the one I'd been able to see ever since I was little.

Agent Elus set about having me taught, for a start. Sometimes he'd come in and teach me himself, when he hadn't nothing better to do, which wasn't often. A lot of the time he had a machine do it – which made me jump first up, I'll tell you for a true fact. Figure a clothes mangle or a well windlass was about as clever a machine as I was used to, and then you'll maybe have an idea what it was like when Elus sat me down with a box that could talk to me, show me pictures, even answer questions.

It turned out that "ignorant" and "stupid" ain't the same thing. There was so much I didn't know, I didn't even know it. Like there was a place some kilometres up where the air just stopped – not all at once, but over a distance – and above there was called "space" and no-one could live there, except they could with another machine to help them. Like "Coriolis" was a huge machine thousands of kilometres high, and it never fell down 'cos it was too busy falling sideways, though it didn't look like it on account of the whole planet was spinning sideways. Like the world itself was a big ball like a bowling ball ten thousand kilometres across, only ten thousand kilometres wasn't even peanuts to the distance to the sun and the stars, which were all suns themselves.

There was a lot of lessons like that, but it wasn't all sitting down and learning stuff from a machine, or even from Agent Elus. He fixed it up with me to go learn about how to drive a land machine, a "sand buggy" he called it, with a lady called Janeen, though she wasn't that much older'n me. A sand buggy had four wheels, bigger and fatter than the cart wheels I'd been used to, made of some off-world stuff called "rubber" and pumped full of air, which seemed a lot like magic for a start but which sure worked well. The buggy had a kind of a yoke bar to hold onto and to make it go the way you wanted, and a couple of little levers you pushed with your feet to make it go faster or slow. Janeen got me to drive it round a big patch of sand they had next to the spaceport, slow at first until I got the way of it, then faster until I was pushing it as quick as it would go.

After a bit there got to be some other kids taking the same kind of training as I was. We didn't talk much about where we'd come from or how we got here, but you can figure anyone who had a safe home and a good future was going to be staying put and not footslogging a thousand kilometres looking for men from the moon. There didn't seem to be much need to ask for more of a story.

So I got to learning that there was a whole bunch of other worlds up there round a load of the lights in the sky, and a lot of 'em were a nicer place to live than Qudira. I found out what a colony world was – how it meant my great-to-a-lot grandfolks came to this place hundreds of years ago to set up a new home – and I got to thinking things through about how the new home had turned out to be such a craphole.

Some places up there, they said, were run like businesses, or had a whole-world government where everyone had a say in what the laws would be. Some were run by a kind of committee, or even one tough guy and his hangers-on, and some worlds were split up into big countries with their own government, or maybe had a bunch of tough guys ruling a few hundred square kilometres each.

And down at the bottom was us. No-one ran a damned thing, and every time someone started to make it better, someone else bust it up again.

* * *

Whenever I meet someone who thinks anarchy is good, I want to beat the stupid out of them with a lead pipe.

There are kids that live on some world that's too rich for their own good that get to thinking how unfair it is that folks want to stop them doing what they want. There are some folks that are old enough to know better that think that human beings should be let alone to do as they want, when they want, and somehow everything will work out just fine. If it was up to me, I'd ship 'em off to Qudira with ten hectares and a mule, an' if they were in any state to do so, they'd be begging to be let off again before a season was gone.

Agent Elus sat down with us kids one time and we talked it all through. All of us – and I said, most of us weren't sharing much of a story and didn't need to – knew darned well what it meant to live in a place with no government. We hardly guessed what it was like to live in any of the other places, but we knew why everyone we ever heard of was stuck like a cow in a mud-hole. It was because as soon as anyone had anything worth taking, someone came along and took it, and there wasn't a thing anyone could do about it.

Oh, sometimes a bunch of farmers would get together and try to stand up to them, but they had damn little to fight with, and if they did get their hands on any weapons, then after the bandits had rolled right over them anyway, they'd take the weapons along with them for next time.

GalCop did its best to stop things getting worse, but GalCop had problems of its own. Seems like half the galaxy was caught up in the same kind of mess – planet by planet was doing OK for itself, but when you looked at the bigger picture, the only forces that were trying to keep the whole thing running along were up against the same problems Qudira had. There wasn't a galaxy government, the strong planets had all they could do to keep their own places running, and there was a lot of folks more than willing to just take whatever they could.

We picked up this kind of stuff along of learning to work machines of one kind or another. Vehicles mostly, but plenty else besides – I even learned to do a little engineering of my own, much good may it do me if ever my Sidewinder packs up on me somewhere out between the systems, but it felt good to pick up a skill like that – and also weapons of one sort or another. There was long guns and shotguns as well as the kind I owned, all to help us learn to pick up a target near or far away, quick enough to get a shot in while it would do the most good. I was good with all of them, as it turned out, especially with the long guns and far-away targets. Agent Elus watched, smiled and nodded, and made notes.

What felt real good, though, was feeling like we could

make a difference. We wanted to know how we could help our own world, for a start, 'cos it was no accident it was such a hellhole. People worked hard to keep it that way. There were the Mister Bigs pulling the strings, and their puppets went all the way down to the Fat Hannahs and beyond.

When my old-timer dropped me a hint about kids being taken off to Coriolis and never seen again, he was too near the truth by half. The reason, as I was picking up on, was money. A few human beings – or some other species from some worlds not even all that far away – packed up in a cargo barrel can be shipped off to the back end of the galaxy, or even just a star system over, and if the market's right at the time you can make real money on the deal. The crazy pills and the like can net you even more – or else they can be used to get kids into the slave barrels in the first place or the kind of deal Agent Elus sketched out in Fat Hannah's. I asked him one time what he meant by "do anything, no matter what your momma told you," and he just grinned.

"You're old enough to figure it out," he said. "Engage your brain."

"You mean… say it was me, and I needed that stuff, I might even…" I finished the sentence, but I ain't going to now.

"That's about the least of what you'd do."

"But… well, surely I wouldn't…" I said, mentioning something someone once told me real bad girls might do.

"By the second day, you'd be more than willing. And after the first couple of times, you'd think nothing of it if it meant getting your next yellow rock – and you'd still not have hit bottom."

It takes a lot to make me blush, but right there and then I was glad nobody else was there. "Do people ever…?"

"End of the third day, you'd make like you enjoyed it if that's what the customer wanted. 'Course, you might be in competition with the boys for that, so it'd be a case of whoever looked the most eager."

So sometimes, when we've been hit by a pirate convoy,

and I figure what might already be in a Python's holds if he's willing to blow up an honest trader for plunder, I don't find it hard to run my laser down his spine until he blows. That, mind you, is without even figuring how the guns get into the hands of the bandits – which is the third leg of how they keep a place like Qudira down in the mud.

* * *

Once you've seen your homeworld from space, there's no going back.

Again, 'cos it's so easy to forget I sometimes forget it myself, I'd spent my whole life thinking maybe the valley we lived in and the volcanoes smoking up the horizon was all there was. Anyone who's had a flatscreen or a computer about the place all their life will know at least what shape their whole planet is, and maybe a whole lot about who lives where on their own world. In plenty of places they'll know all about space travel and what comes through the Coriolis station, who their neighbours are in the next system over. On the higher-tech worlds, as I learned later, you can still be real young and know that there are eight sectors in the Galaxy and how GalCop rates 'em all according to how they're run and what they do to make a living. Then you start to understand how things are shipped from place to place – and how they have to be, to keep the whole show moving.

There's a smallish patch of land, near the ground station – twenty-thirty kilometres out from it, maybe, and probably no further – where they're really straining everything to get Qudira on the up and up. They get some fancy goods in from off world, computers and smart machines, to try to modernise the farming and so on, and the goods they can freight out pays for what comes in and means it can be built on later. If they can keep that going for long enough, maybe Qudira might be a better place to live.

Sad part is, though, that here like everywhere else

they've still to look out for the ruiners – the ones who don't care what kind of a future Qudira might have tomorrow if they can score themselves some loot today. And the pirate gangs that hang around in the system are just fine with this, 'cos the less Qudira can do about policing its own space, the more they can pillage whoever comes in with the expensive stuff. As below, so above, you might say.

Of course, figuring what I said about ignorance a little while ago, you can guess a lot of the bandits planet-side don't even twig this, and the space pirates sure aren't in any hurry to tell them. Happy to slip a trader through with a few tons of guns they can slip past customs, for sure, and get them sold on to the ground bandits for ready cash and keeping the cycle going – yeah, they'll do that. And that's how innocent families get to be dead, and, thanks to karma, how someone like me gets to be in space looking out for what she can do to break the cycle.

It wasn't until we'd been several months in training that Agent Elus took us off-world for the first time. We'd had all sorts of exercises to sharpen our balance, our aim, our sense of direction, and as much as we could learn about piloting skills as we could learn while still ground-bound. Some worlds had air vehicles we coulda tried out, Agent Elus said, but we didn't have the base facilities to keep 'em airworthy on Qudira. So on four wheels, three or two, over rocks or over sand, we learned what we could that way. Some of it – like how to pick yourself out of the dust when you'd stacked your sand-buggy trying for more speed than was smart right then and there, and not mind the pain or even the broken arm too much – taught us guts, I guess, but wouldn't be much use to us in a spacecraft. In a Sidewinder, or anything similar, you mainly don't get hurt. You either get dead, or you come back fully fit with barely even a scorch.

Still, like I say, one day Agent Elus got us all packed into a shuttle that was bound for orbit. We were crammed into the cargo hold along with twenty-nine standard cargo canisters, or TeeCees as I heard they were called, standing room only but at least with something to hold onto. The ride was smoother than I expected, but we'd been warned that some of us were going to barf when we felt free fall for the first time.

There wasn't too much of that – the shuttle's drive was on nearly all of the way up – but a few of us tossed our cookies when the ship had to wait to dock. There wasn't a viewport in the hold, obviously, but there was a flatscreen hooked up to the shuttle's forward view so we got a good look at the Coriolis station for the first time. That, even allowing for the pictures we'd been shown before, was about enough to blow your mind.

It's almost beyond belief that anything made with hands can be so big, so regular, so obviously heavy but hanging there in space with nothing holding it up, and spinning slowly but non-stop, at least until we got close in and the shuttle started rotating too. But even the view of the Coriolis station paled when I got my first look at Qudira from a few thousand klicks up in space. The whole world looks small and precious from up there, and if you peer real close you can see the line between light and dark creeping across the world and you realize that from up here you can see someone's day and someone else's night at the same time.

You even forget about the volcanoes and the storms, never mind what people are doing to each other down there. All you know is that there's this big, beautiful and somehow fragile thing, almost so close you could touch it.

I knew then and there that what I most wanted to do was find a way to stop the whole planet hurting, and whatever we were being trained for was going to make it possible.

* * *

They let the kids in the spacers' bar. Once.

The guy escorting us made a big play of tapping on the intercom and yelling "Children coming in! Everybody decent!" but I guessed at the time this was just for show. Now I know that's so, 'cos I've been on the other side once or twice and if there was anything indecent going on, it would take more than a half minute to get everything ship-shape and fit for kids to see.

Sometimes there's reason enough. There was a time our convoy just hit the Witchpoint and we were hardly getting our formation reset when a bunch of allsorts – Cobras of both kinds, Mambas, a Fer-de-Lance looking like it was running the show – bounced us. From the chatter it seemed like the freighter was carrying someone that someone else wanted rubbed out and could pay real high to see it done. They took out one of us, a newbie in a Gecko on her first run, straight away while she was trying to figure out why all the hostiles were reading "Clean" on her bounty-meter, but we didn't stop to shed any tears and once we'd lit up a Cobra I and the Ferdy was starting to take lots of hits, they all burned witchfuel out of there.

Which was when the regular pirates turned up.

Like I said earlier, sometimes both sides know how to count. This time, the bogeys must've not counted the three or four of us that were still slamming the door on the Assassins' tails when they decided it was worth a go. And, unfortunately, for the short but still too long time it took for us to get back, it pretty much was.

Well – happier times, before I pull up the rest of that memory. It's good to be a youngster full of the thrills of space, rubbing shoulders with some tough guys and gals and, for that matter, some stranger creatures altogether. I'd spent my whole life not knowing that, just a day and a half away by spaceship, there was a whole planet full of creatures that looked kind of like us but smaller and covered in blue fur. And it didn't stop at furry creatures, by a long way.

They made us good and welcome, though they didn't talk much shop in front of us – they spoke plenty about the places they'd been and the sights they'd seen, instead. And when they kicked us out, in the nicest possible way, so they could get on with their R&R in peace, there was still plenty to see.

For a bunch of youngsters fresh off the most backward backwater in the whole sector – and right on the bottom rung of the whole Eight – just being on a Coriolis station was the adventure of a lifetime. To begin with, there were the viewports where you could watch the ships coming in and going out, and the docking bay itself where there was a place for greenhorns to watch the ships being worked on and loaded without getting under anyone's feet. Even the stores they had Space-side were out of this world in every sense as well as the obvious one, with all kinds of fancy goods that I'd never even imagined existed.

But you can't get too hung up on the toy stores when you know you're going to be a spacer. That would all have been very well when you were a little younger, but now you're all grown up you've got your dignity to mind, especially in front of all the traders and couriers and Navy pilots and all the rest of them. None of us said so in as many words, but I guessed we were all thinking pretty much the same thing.

Agent Elus gave us some time to take in all the sights, but he had a for-real trip in space lined up for us, and not just in a station-to-ground crawler at that but a ship that could Witch-jump, though she wasn't going to today – yes, and that was armed like a fighting ship too. He didn't need to tell us what she was. By this time we'd practised our ship recognition enough that we could spot a Cobra Mk III on sight.

Close to, she looked huge, although we'd learn she was a midget next to some, and she was fully loaded with missiles and a big laser front and rear, just so we would know what firepower looked like close up. No cargo hold for us this time; there was space for us all in the crew cockpit, though we had to squeeze up tight.

There isn't any way to describe what it's like to launch from a Coriolis Station in an actual spaceship for the first time, especially when six months ago you'd never seen anything more advanced than a farm cart. If you want to know what it's like, go and try it. If you're not able to, then you don't need me to wring your heart out for you by describing what you can't ever have.

If it makes you feel any better, you'll also never know what it's like to limp into a station with the one other survivor of your whole convoy, knowing that despite your best efforts your freighter bought the farm on this run along with the rest of your wingmates, and you still have to find yourself another job as soon as may be, because that's what you do and it's all you can do to try to make the whole Galaxy a little bit less of a crapsack.

It's at times like that you're just as glad that the spacers' bar is an intensely private club. Once the door's shut behind you, you can indulge in as much grief as it takes to get over the worst day of your life so far. The other spacers in the bar won't respect you the less for it. They know.

*   *   *

Half a minute is a real long time in a space battle.

It doesn't make much odds whether you've been pulled half a minute away from where the action is going down all over again, or whether that's the time you need for your laser to cool down before you can give it a sustained-fire burst on the centre of mass. Sometimes you get both at once, which I guess is more economical because while you're catching up with the furball your laser is cooling anyway. Lasers cool quickly on account of the temperature, but they have to radiate all their heat away into space. Groundside weapons can use air-cooling or even water-cooling, but neither of those works right in space.

Again, that's what an education does for you. The theory lessons carried on while we were on the Coriolis station – and they had even better facilities there than they did groundside, because no matter what might happen on the planet's surface, an orbital station's pretty much invulnerable. You don't need worry about losing a million credits' worth of training college when you're a few thousand klicks above any planet, still less when it's a backwards place that's barely got past the sticks and stones level.

We got caught up on the basics of science. The modes of heat transference took a day or two plus some simple demonstrations to cover, and we pretty soon added in Boltzmann's Law although I will never understand the mathematics if I study it till the day I die. They threw in electronics, laws of gravity and motion, and a whole lot more besides, not to mention enough economics that we could understand what all these ships ferrying stuff from place to place were trying to do.

If it'd been possible to run the galaxy like one of the best-run planets, there'd've been Government ships taking things from where they were in plenty to where they didn't have enough, and everyone would be living the good life on the strength of it. At least, that's how it looked to me. Even somewhere like Qudira can make something someone wants, and even if it takes fifty tons of exported food to buy a ton of computer gear in return, it all works out fair in the end. A planet that starts to get what it needs to modernise can make more of what it's selling, buy more of what it needs, and so on up and up. That's how I understood the economics classes, anyway.

But none of this works quite as it should without a galactic government, when everything that's going to get done only happens because someone's making enough money to see that it does happen... and there are too many people who can see a quicker and dirtier way to make a profit.

Which is where I come to be barrelling towards my freighter as fast as I can hustle, and there is only one top speed for any given combination of hull and drive. It helps a mite that I'm only about forty-five kilos, fifty dressed ready for action, but it's only a fleabite when you count everything else. My computer's spotting me targets as fast as I can lock 'em on, but it's down to me to make my shots count and all I can do is hope that I'm shooting the guys most in need of shooting.

I open up at the full fifteen k's that an Ingram M1928A2 will carry and I hit what I mean to hit. That's my particular strength that they identified in training and that I've worked on ever since. I burn away the Cobra One's rear shield in moments and I'm searing through the hull while he's still panicking and trying to get a missile lock on me. I know what to expect and I cut my speed right down the instant I see a blue-white trace coming in, getting on the horn and calling "Can you ECM please, Mother?" Thankfully my freighter responds in seconds while I'm still trying to sight on the missile. Sidewinders can't carry countermeasures, rear lasers or fuel injection, which means you have to nail a missile on the run-in or hope you can get out of range before it catches you. And although I score over 80% in simulated missile shoot-downs, that's not the kind of odds that's going to keep you alive.

As soon as I hear the computer announce "Counter-measures", I trust to my luck that it's not a hardpoint and even as I'm opening the taps again I see the missile blow. I'm already looking for my next target while I'm scolding my laser for not cooling down quicker, and I have plenty of choice and too few wingmen. That half a minute cost us – and I'm not dead sure the Assassins aren't still sharking around out there, waiting for the fur to stop flying so they can earn their pay after all.

I spot a Gecko in need of attention. He's slower than me but can turn at least as tight, maybe tighter if he's good at his work, and once again I open up at maximum range and scorch him good and hard before he breaks, shedding enough plasma to show he's hurt but still in the fight, and now my laser's right in the red zone and I don't have any other firepower. He's figured that his best chance is to turn and try to cook me before I can finish him, and I pull around as tight as I can and put him directly sternwards where he'll find the thinnest target I can give him. The odd shot tells, but I'm still doing OK and watching the laser cool until I can turn and give him another burst. He's decided it's time to use the one missile he's packing, and once again I'm asking my freighter to blow it for me.

And my gut wrenches when I hear the silence.

* * *

Different pilots are suited to different ships.

That didn't ought to surprise anyone. Figure all the trainees in my group were the best Agent Elus had found on

Qudira, it stands to reason that amongst ourselves some would have better aim, some faster reflexes, some better tactical sense and some a better head for where they are and where they want to be.

To begin with we were all just cutting our teeth on a simple, basic spaceship that would get us out into the system and back to the Coriolis station after some exercises. The best facilities in the sector were at Lave – but that was almost a whole sector away, and what we had were nearly as good.

By now we weren't at Qudira any more. We were over at Tianve, just about eight light-years over – and I was educated enough to know what that meant, both in scientific terms and in the practicals of how long it took to get there in Witch-space. Too far for a single jump, but you could get there in just over two days with a refuelling stop at Malama. Tianve had almost the best tech in the whole sector, and the only reason, Agent Elus remarked, that it didn't have the beating of Lave was that the locals wouldn't vote us enough money. GalCop and the Navy between them funded the training facilities, but over at Lave the planet chipped in with a big contribution on the Factor's say-so. That more than made up for the fact that Lave's fancy kit had to be shipped in from several systems over.

However that might be, we had plenty to do, first of all going out with an instructor in a two-seat ship to check that all the hard work we'd done in the simulator paid off, until she was sure that we weren't going to splash ourselves all over a buoy or, worse, all over the front of Tianve station. Then, after a training run had gone real well, she took us back into the docking bay, opened the hatch, and said "Take her out to the nav buoy and bring her back in one piece."

Not much of a mission for your first solo in a real ship, but it's still enough to give you the fidgets when you call for clearance, set yourself to go out the launch tube, get clear of the docking corridor and then head out to round the buoy. Once you're used to how everything works you might as well get a lock through your rear view, call the station and ask for clearance straight away, because you've more than enough time to get round the buoy and back into the station in your two minutes in a fast ship. I for sure didn't, though.

Later on I'd get used to handling a fast ship, not just rounding buoys but in combat, although a Sidie isn't fast enough to outrun a missile. You can keep it chasing you until its motor runs out and it self-destructs, though, provided you're quick enough on the turn when it gets in real close. That's not something you want to do very many times in your life, though. Practise it in the sim, sure, or with a dummy warhead. That's a whole heap safer and you'd have to ram it head-on going fast to hurt yourself much that way. Out in realspace, though, you save that for emergencies, like when you've called your freighter for ECM and not even gotten a negative by way of courtesy.

I had to put up with that damn Gecko chasing me while I was at it, but I didn't have too much to worry about there. Pulling the kind of high-gee random turns it takes to keep a missile from impacting you mostly makes you a hard target for laser fire, even for a tight-turning ship like a Gecko. It was longer than I liked before the missile blew, but when it did I had my laser fully cooled down as a bonus, and I figured I had that Gecko on toast.

I was also worried it was too late to matter. I was dead right.

Where my freighter should have been was just a cloud of gently-scattering cargo containers, with a Python slithering in to scoop them up and still three of his escorts showing red on my screen. Just the one trace, which was Terek in his Mamba, the *You Shouldn't Have Done That*. Not as fast or agile as my Sidewinder, but tough and capable for its size. I signalled him.

"Screw the odds. If they go home, we don't."

We hunted down the escorts one by one. They should've been at least as good as we were, with the numbers on their side and the chance of some covering fire from their mother. Maybe we just wanted it worse than they did.

When the going got too rough, the Python Witched out

of there. We didn't even think twice before following him. Then… Well, he should have shelled out for a better rear laser. He tagged both of us, one after the other, screaming for help all the while, but there wasn't any. He screamed something about lackeys of the Party and dying for the Liberation before he went, too. You can guess how much we cared.

After we'd blown him up, we set ourselves for the Coriolis station in our new system. We fell in with a Boa and her escorts, which made for a slower trip than we'd planned, but we weren't complaining. There was plenty to drink that nightcycle, but no girls, not for us – and the other spacers left us to our drunk.

Eventually Terek slurred, "Time to hit the sack. I don't want to be alone tonight. You?"

"Me either. But you know I like girls best?" I smiled, kinda sadly.

He chuckled tiredly. "If it comes to that," he said, "I like boys best."

* * *

"Your median life expectancy will be one minute."

That's the kind of quote that gets you to sit up and pay attention, believe me. Our new lecturer was a guy called Anli Hadd'zi, a sleepy-looking humanoid a little taller than we were and a brighter shade of yellow than a pure human coulda been while not actually being dead. But he spoke few words and to the point, and he had graphs and figures and so on to back up what he said.

"That's timed from the first time you see a red trace," Hadd'zi added. "I don't count launch up to Witchspace exit, which could give you forty-nine hours in the cockpit before anything goes down. Once the trouble starts – One minute. We're doing all we can to push that figure up. The data don't lie, though."

He popped a chart up on the wall. There was a blinking

red line just a minute along the time axis. To the left, a whole bunch of dots. To the right… then the dots started to get spread out a bit more.

"As you can see, the half of you that live through that first minute have a brighter future. At that point you have a fair chance of surviving the whole fight. Next time round, you're not so green any more. You're odds-on to get through your next one okay. And so on up. Pilots that have seen a whole lot of successful missions aren't rare. But you have to live through that first minute."

This was a come-down after the first thrill of learning that we were going to be sponsored to a real live fighting ship all of our very own to go off in, have adventures, and help to make the galaxy a better place for everyone. They'd bumped me up to an actual Sidewinder by now, with a live laser and all, because it wasn't a given that even the outer fringes of Tianve system were dead safe. There was a rumour that there were hired killers out there looking for trainees to pick off. Figures that if we were out to spoil some criminal's fun in the future, he might be looking to do some spoiling of his own first, before we'd got properly trained. That one-minute statistic would be starting to look kinda hopeful if we got bounced while we were still training, but at least with a proper laser we wouldn't be sitting targets.

That Sidewinder was going to be my very own provided I passed out of training OK and didn't want to go home to Qudira. There wasn't much chance of that. Even if I'd had a home and farm to go back to, once I'd seen what space life had to offer, there was no contest. The medical care was way better, for a start.

"You'll want the baby shot, of course?" the doctor said. She looked even younger than me, but the ID on the surgery wall had her holo as well as her degrees, so I guess they get schooled real good real young on Xexedi. She already had her hypo loaded with about fifty different immunity formulae and I didn't see the need for another one, and I said so.

"Don't see why I'd need it. Just between us, I won't be

getting up to stuff with any guys, if you know what I mean."

"Sure. But there's a steady trickle of girls I get through here who weren't going to be getting up to stuff, only it turns out they did, after all, and now they've got something that needs taking care of. You can get that done at any GalCop station no matter the local tech, but there isn't a doctor in all the Eight can guarantee that your body or your brain will be quite what they would have been if it hadn't needed doing," she said.

It was surprising how little visible tech there was in the doctor's office. Even her instrument case was small and portable, and everything in it might have been a metal stick for all I could tell different. I guess she'd brought it with her from Xexedi. They can do about anything there except turn ships invisible – and I hear rumour they're working on that. Her class holo was next to her degree. Nearly everyone in it was a green frog, but I knew better by now than to sell them short on that account.

"Well... okay," I said, studying the infopad she'd handed me. Turns out it's one shot, fire and forget, reversible any time with a hundred percent success... which was pure magic compared to what I'd grown up with. I wasn't planning on needing it, but there literally wasn't a downside that I could see.

And that way you do get to be covered for those times when you've already committed yourself to something before you take your sober pill, and it would be heartless to get cold feet even if you actually wanted to.

I really didn't want to sleep alone and nor did Terek, and we did sleep, but that wasn't all we did, and in the morning when we woke up next to each other neither of us screamed. He gave a little laugh, and so did I.

"I think I still prefer girls," I said.

"I think I still prefer boys."

I yawned and stretched. "You think we ought to make sure?"

So we made sure. We made good and sure, with no half

measures, and I reached a couple of important conclusions: firstly, that boys weren't that bad after all when you really, really didn't want to sleep alone, and secondly, that the doctor had the right of it.

Once we were up and about again it was business as usual, which meant we were both looking to get hired and neither of us had any difficulty finding a hirer. And just for once, we had a complete milk run.

* * *

Sooner or later the training is over.

Maybe it's true for everyone in every occupation, but it's certainly true in mine: the day you have to put up and show that you're ready to practise your trade for real always comes too soon. I couldn't get that one-minute statistic out of my head, and anyone who wasn't worried by it would have to be an idiot.

We all left Tianve by one means or another. In my case Agent Elus was off to Aate for some leave, and he'd hired himself a passage aboard a Cobra Mk III with a fancy passenger cabin and a hot-shot pilot. For all that he figured it was worth taking a couple of us along as escort, which meant me and a kid called Ramiss, another Sidewinder pilot. It was a two-jump trip by way of Inines, a hi-tech Communist system where the Cobra stopped at a fuel station to top off tanks rather than slog down to the main station. Communists mainly keep the pirates and assassins out, with not much help from GalCop, but you have to grind through a lot of traffic. The mining ships and workers' transports make up a lot of that, and they are slow with a capital Yawn.

Aate was a come-down after the excitements of Tianve, although it was a few dozen steps up the long ladder compared to home, and the Coriolis station had the usual amusements. The spacers were polite but firm; until we'd seen the elephant (and I looked one up on the computer and couldn't believe such a funny creature ever existed anywhere) we could have one drink in the bar and then go to our rooms until we got word that someone was hiring. That actually took a day or two. Traffic through Aate was fairly slack, since the profits were likely to be bigger elsewhere – some die-hards were still running computers into Qudira, I heard, but they were mainly looking to buy them cheaper at Esbiza or Malama.

Sooner or later, though, you get someone wanting some company for a trip they have planned. That's the only way a Sidewinder gets to leave a star system – though you can hitch a lift through someone's wormhole if you don't mind them looking at you funny. Ramiss and I both had our names down on the list and I'll give the spacers this, they didn't try to stop us taking our fair turn. There was no guarantee we'd get hired together, and as it turned out, we didn't.

You don't often make two trips in a row with the same partners, and at the most you might have noticed who was coming up on the cab rank next to you and maybe got to know them the nightcycle before you launched. It was well out of the ordinary when Terek and I actually made three trips in a row together, and after the shock of losing our freighter one trip, the fact that we made it through the next one without a sniff of trouble left us figuring it was party time.

Our trader captain made no bones about paying us; we get the same whether the other side turn up for a fight or not, and if you've just dropped off a big cargo and pocketed a bundle of credits, I guess you don't mind paying your hired guns whether they've had to earn their keep or just been a good-luck charm. The worst you could say about this trip was that *Nuclear Nellie*, an Anaconda, couldn't have gone any slower without being fitted with retro-rockets. What she was delivering I don't know, but even with her auto-loaders running flat out they had the dock tied up a long time. Not that I was hanging around to watch the unloading, not while it was party time – and believe me, right then and there it was party time.

I'm not really sure what the girls in the spacers' bar actually do for a living. I've never out-and-out paid one for a thing, and while I don't mind standing treat for a bottle or two and maybe some tasty eats, you'd never be able to retire on it. On the other hand, there's plenty of legitimate business around a Coriolis station and for all I know they all work the make-up bars and novelty stores by day. Is it very terrible of me that as a rule I don't ask?

There don't seem to be bar-boys on the same scale, but you generally find that a few spacers on any station are like Terek – happiest with each other's company. The girls who like boys would be the worst off, except that most boy spacers prefer girls and a girl spacer doesn't have to do more than ask, even with the local competition.

Well, I found myself a hot little piece, a little shorter than me with pale hair in tight ringlets, slim but stacked in the right places, and we set ourselves to have a fun time. I say they don't pay us enough, but that's not to say it's ever hard to pay a bar bill, and I never hit a spacers' bar yet that didn't have a few treats I'd never seen before. This one had actual gold flakes floating in it, and was priced accordingly.

Some party girls like other girls naturally, some are too good-mannered to say no, and this one, whichever way you slice it, was well worth an evening spent listening to her prattle. By rights I ought to have slept right through my alarm call – and yet I found myself wide awake hours before local dawn, cold sober but with my head spinning round.

I slipped out of my apartment and found another one close by. I tapped the buzzer. "Terek? Got company?"

He grunted – but spacers wake up quick. "Not any more."

"You have now," I said, trying not to cry. "Open up, will you?"

* * *

I lasted more than a minute in my first fight.

That ain't gonna surprise any of you who are reading

this. I guess I was lucky it didn't take very long for my first time to happen. There were three of us, two Mambas who'd seen a fight or two and myself, as green as Leestian evil juice, along of a Python Clipper, a newish looking ship that spanked along a fair bit quicker than the old rustbuckets – and it was all the Mambas could do to keep up with her at full stretch, too. What the Clipper was freighting was none of my business, but the big money into Esbiza, where we were headed, is in furs or any kind of good-class hooch.

We'd left the Witchpoint a few seconds behind us and our freighter was scanning for any friendlies who might be heading down towards the station or, failing that, any local police. Esbiza's not the worst, but the planetary governments – they've got two main ones, and another six or seven looking for a bigger piece of the pie – don't always haul on the same trace, so the law can be spotty. What we were actually seeing was laser fire in the distance, and not the little flashes you get that tell you a miner's just blasting rock, either. Also the automatics very kindly told us that the goonies were unusually active at the time, which it helps to know.

One of the Mambas, *Predator's Downfall*, signalled to keep the formation tight. I'd've been happier if there'd been a few more of us, but that's the trader's call and I wasn't turning down paying work. I just did as I'd been briefed, tucking in on the right flank outboard of and behind *Can I Just Interrupt?*, the other Mamba, and we waited for the trouble to start.

Pirates have gotten cheeky these days, they tell me. Time was when they didn't just up and demand cargo with menaces – they'd aim to get the drop on a convoy and vape most of the escorts straight off if they could, then if the freighter started dumping TeeCees they might stop and scoop 'em if they felt like it. That was before my time. They say that in those days the pirate ambushes were just too obvious for words, and they hadn't time to stop and chat if they hoped to score any kills. These days, they work together better, and figure they've got enough of an edge they can get mouthy.

Well, our Clipper started towards the station as hot as she could trot, with us tagging along but waiting our moment to break to left and right and pincer them. It was the usual mob of pirates, not too well-to-do since they still had a couple of Kraits in the line-up, and they're dead out of fashion these days; and they had a rustbucket along to scoop the cargo, maybe figuring that if they scored enough booty they could trade her in for something a bit more up-to-date later. Of course, we aimed to stop that.

Chances are that *Downfall* and *Can I?* were watching my back as we went in, but I didn't have time to notice, with my heart trying to thump its way out of my chest and my bladder telling me it was a good job I was wearing spacer's pants. The nanofibre's well worth the money and keeps you dry and fresh whether it's just been too long since you last got to civilised facilities or the nerves have got too much. I locked on to one of the Kraits and lit him up just like I'd been trained to, listening for the audio to confirm that my laser was hitting his shields.

The only thing he had going for him was that his energy could recharge quicker than mine. Otherwise, I had him going and coming – beaten for speed and on the turn. He tried to lose me in a turning fight, and my laser was close to the redline as I took whatever shots I could when it looked like I was either on or pulling just enough lead that he'd fly through my beam. Then he started plasma-shedding and just tried to high-tail it out of there. A Krait can't outrun a Sidewinder, though. I eased off the speed, checking my six again and again, until my laser was cool enough for a worthwhile burst, and then I ran him through.

According to the log it was then ninety-three seconds since the red traces appeared, so that put me more'n half a minute over the median survival time, for which I was duly thankful. The other two escorts had accounted for another goonie apiece, and that was their cue to snarl something about it not being worth it and light out for the remote reaches. We let 'em go. We were hired to escort our freighter, not to wipe out every last pirate in the system.

It seemed all so simple then – a lot simpler than when I was lying in Terek's bunk and trying not be be a silly little girl all over him, but I wanted his arms around me and I couldn't even give one simple reason why. Put it down to a whole bundle of different reasons.

There's the thing they call "Survivor's Guilt", which happens to anyone who's lived through something that killed off some of those closest to them. Hired guns get it worse than most, because we're meant to see that our freighter gets through, and if we weren't a hundred percent committed to that then we'd be in another job. There was the part where I was replaying that "If they go home, we don't" routine in my head and realizing at that moment I really didn't care about staying alive. There was even the bit about how I was getting to realize that boys weren't bad after all – especially one in particular.

* * *

There are times when you just feel so grown up.

For me it was the huge relief that came with realizing I'd gotten into a for-real space combat and come out the winner, without even a scratch on my ship. It had all been so surprisingly easy, too, which kinda led me to hope it was always going to be as easy as that. Of course, the other spacers were quick to put me straight.

But they didn't bust my bubble first off. Once we'd hit the station and the Clipper was off-loading, we hit the bar and let it be known that there was a new pilot on the block, one who wasn't green any more. Of course I was still rated Harmless. It takes several trips to lose that – at least, you'd better hope it did, because who needs to get into eight separate duels on one mission? There are some who do it, of course – the galaxy's a big place – but there are plenty more who buy the farm because they got into more fights than they were ready for in one go.

After I'd been made officially free of every spacers' bar

in the Eight, with a short ceremony and a ritual handing-over of a little plaque they keep behind the counter, I sat nursing my drink for quite a long while. Of course you have to understand that just having the right of entry didn't mean I ranked up there with all the seasoned campaigners. There's a pecking order that you don't ignore, and while there's no official insignia to show who's Dangerous and who's still Poor, there are conventions that let those who need to know recognise the signs. If you ever see someone wearing a laser crystal in their hair, for instance, you need to be real respectful. By the same token, if you make the mistake of wearing one yourself when your record shows less than a thousand kills, be prepared to be in for bad trouble the moment someone checks up on you.

But I wasn't thinking about that so much, and after a while Taniqua, out of *Predator's Downfall*, detached herself from the little group she was with and set herself down by me.

"Why so thoughtful?"

It was a natural question, and it deserved a polite answer, but all I could manage was "Thinking about medians."

She'd obviously heard the same statistic I had. There was a hint of impatience in her head-toss, which had a snort to go with it. "Maths isn't all it's cracked up to be. Once you've used up your first minute, it doesn't mean you're running on borrowed time."

"I know," I said. "It's just… odds are good that half the people I trained with didn't get through that minute, and it's less than a standard week since I last saw them."

Taniqua took in half the bar with a sweep of her arm. "Welcome to our world, kid. Odds are also good that you'll never see any of these good people here again after tomorrow. Not that they're all going to become someone's statistic, but it's a big galaxy and it can take a long time before your paths cross again, let alone in the same system. If it makes you feel better, tell yourself everyone's alive until you've heard proof to the contrary. You may never be proved wrong."

"I guess I can do that," I shrugged, and gave her a

brave half-smile.

"That's the spirit. And meanwhile, you've earned your pay for today, so spend a small fraction of it partying hard. Eat and drink, for tomorrow it may be your turn in the barrel."

I asked her to explain that one to me and she told me a filthy story about men on a ship, the kind that goes on water. Then she laughed and said, "But we can do better for ourselves than that. Go on, have a few drinks, then jump on a cute guy. It's what you deserve."

With just the hint of a blush I explained that I'd never been with a man and wasn't at all sure I ever wanted to, but it just made her laugh again. "Well, a girl then. There's plenty of choice. Or get your cross-species freak on if that's what lights your fuse. You won't be the only one."

I followed her gaze across the bar to where a black Cat a little smaller than me was rubbing up against a guy with a little Asp-shaped badge on his tunic. Asp pilots swagger like no-one's business, on account of having massive firepower and hyperspace capability. This one, though, was scratching the Cat's back like he meant business.

"She's from Diso," said Taniqua, "and when she arches her back like that, it's not a saucer of milk she's begging for. Good luck to the pair of them figuring out who's gonna do what with what, but you can bet your boots something's happening tonight, 'cos she's a whole sector away from home and it's her night to yowl."

I thought it over and guess Taniqua maybe had a point, and most times it worked out pretty well, then and later. Which was all fine and dandy until I found myself clinging to Terek in the small hours, feeling far more attached to another spacer than it's real smart to get in our business, and doing a bad job of explaining why.

It's not good to get attached. You need a clear head when you're in a fight – you don't need to be committed to watching one special person's back, nor wondering where they are when they're several star systems away and you're hoping to meet up again. Anli Hadd'zi probably has stats showing how that knocks down your survival chances. I didn't really care.

Maybe Terek saw things differently, though. He held me as long as I wanted, listened to me making no sense – and he was gone in the morning.

*   *   *

Tomorrow it may be your turn in the barrel.

Even I wasn't so naïve as to think every run I went on would be as simple as the first one, and to be honest I was expecting the trouble to start sooner rather than later. But as I stretched, yawned, and rolled out of my cot to grab chow and face the new day, I was feeling cautiously hopeful.

There was a dent in the mattress next to where I'd been sleeping. I felt like someone was bound to notice this glow I was giving off, but I decided not to worry about it. She'd slipped away a little before my alarm went off, giving me a polite peck on the forehead on her way out, and I knew she had her own day to get ready for, even if it didn't mean getting into the seat of a fighting ship and hoping you could shoot straighter and faster than someone else.

Grabbing a bite to eat, I checked the roster board, where everyone's names came up in cab-rank order for whoever was hiring today. Just before me, name and likeness, was the black Cat I'd noticed the previous night – and she was in the chow line just behind me, too. It might've got my face scratched for me if I'd said so, but she looked like she'd had a whole bowl of cream to herself the previous night, and I guess she'd managed to get her yowling done after all even if the soundproofing had kept her from waking everyone else up.

"Hi," she purred, and if that sounds like I'm trying to be funny, all I can say is that's how she sounded. "Name's Maussa. Want to sit together?"

I desperately tried not to crack up when I heard how her name was pronounced. Those hands have opposable thumbs and claws that go all the way back in, but they're not just for decoration. Maussa was smaller and lighter than me, with soft-looking black fur that ached to be petted... and from the little I knew about the various Felines scattered about the Eight, she could make me wish I'd never been born without even breathing hard.

If she wanted to be friendly then I was not going to say no. We found a table with a view of the planet dawn below, which I'd never got tired of from the first time I'd looked down on one on Qudira. "And you arrre...?"

"Marilee, Sidewinder *Get An Honest Job.*" I'd named her myself, which is spacer's privilege no matter how green and even if someone else paid for the ship. Different pilots have different tastes and most of 'em have a kind of a sense of humour even if the wit's not always sparkling. Others –

"Mine's a Sidewinderrr, too. *Pause for Thought.*"

Others, especially trigger-happy Felines who seem to be looking for any excuse for a cat-fight, choose the kind of name that someone's likely to laugh at so they can take offence. The one thing you can say is that they aren't looking to kill you unless you go for a weapon first. They might leave you smarting and with a few days needing some extra meds until the claw-marks heal, but if it's just a casual fight as between equals, the claws don't come all the way out and they don't bite down.

I didn't find this out at the time and I didn't go looking to, either. Maussa had a teasing expression that told me she knew what a rookie I was but that the mischief was going to stop at gentle hazing, and if I was smart I'd let it ride.

We got ourselves signed up with a Python an hour after breakfast, along with three other ships – and he already had a couple more tagging along from his last system. Whatever it was he was up to that might make him such a risk, and however much trouble he might have got into on his last jump, well, those are questions you just don't ask. You can choose for yourself to turn someone down if you don't like his rep or where he's going, but you don't make a habit of that if you want to stay in work.

What the risk might be we found out soon enough. It turned out I was going home – and I knew damn well what that meant by now, especially when our trader let drop that he was carrying computers.

Some of us face up to risks, and some of us run away from them. When I woke up and found Terek gone, it sure felt like he'd run away. Later I'd get to thinking about why he'd do a thing like that, but not straight away. I felt like I'd bared my soul to him and he'd paid me back with a slap in the face.

Whatever the whys and wherefores, I left that station with a bad attitude and a cold intensity I'd not felt before. There wasn't room in our business for a girl to be a silly emotional female? Then there was room to be a ruthlessly efficient ship-killer, and I figured I had just the equipment for that. I didn't much care who I signed up with, I just resolved it was going to be so much the worse for anyone who crossed me.

"Ladies and gentlemen, our target for today is Maesin," read the briefing notes. "Be on your guard for pirates and be aware that we are carrying passengers."

Maesin. A revolting dump, as the guidebook puts it – and with about as much scum and villainy as Qudira, even before you start counting the risk of a contract hit on the passengers. I gave an evil grin I was glad the girl in the next ship couldn't possibly see. I was in a bad mood, and a revolting dump full of pirates and assassins was just what I needed.

* * *

Find out what you do well. Then do it.

That's not a quote from something someone told me; that's all my own work. Maybe it's not so profound as all that, but hey, I do what I can. 'Course, it helps if what you do well is actually good enough to see you through…

And none of this is rolling out and sounding as wise and deep as I'd hoped, which is why I figure I'll stick to being a combat pilot, not a lecturer.

I wasn't yet dead sure that what I do well was good enough. We witched into Qudira system, our trader and his eight escorts, and about ten kilocredits' worth of fancy electronic goods. That was station prices, of course. If you could get a choke on the market and ship 'em in yourself, you could likely ask a lot more than a hundred credits a pop. And even if all you did was filch 'em off the trader and sell them somewhere else, you're still making a tidy profit – plus, maybe, keeping the planet in the mud where you want it. Well, there I was to try to upset that plan, along of half a dozen other singleships that were likely better at it than I was.

How the word gets around among the pirates, I ain't yet learned, but the trouble is that there's only one entry point into a system, to within a few kilometres. The theory's several astrophysics degrees out of my reach, but the only way in is what's called the Witchpoint, which they helpfully mark with a buoy in every system I ever went to. That means, if you're real up-front about what you mean to do to anyone coming in, you can camp close in by the buoy and wait to see who comes through – and with a good computer, they tell me, you can predict people's arrival time to a couple of hours.

So we knew to expect a reception committee, and we got one – Fer-de-Lances, Asps, and a bunch of hangers-on. They broadcast the usual hail they're using these days when they want to bully a freighter captain into giving them an easy payday: "We just want your cargo". Our freighter captain had told us there was no way that was going to happen – he quoted some old poem or other, but what it came down to was this:

Once you've paid off a pirate for threatening you, you've taught him that he can get paid for making threats. This is not a good thing.

So instead we came about into attack position, our freighter too if it came to that. He fancied his chances with his own laser before turning round and letting them chew on his rear shields for a bit – and he was toting another laser aft as well.

Pythons look slow and clumsy, but they can turn good and tight and if they have the rear laser they can catch a lot of suckers.

But for me, I was just looking to get my sights on, same as the first time, only this time someone tagged me first. We'd been trained good. If you're taking hits, don't sit there and squeal about it – pull some evasive manoeuvres and break that target lock, quickly! A military-spec laser will go right through you in just a few seconds if you don't react fast!

With so many other targets around, the one who was tagging me lost interest once I'd broken, and I kept myself weaving and dodging while my regenerators did what they could to balance the energy out again. But you can't just dodge, you have to make yourself useful – and I found myself with a clear shot at one of the Ferdys, a full fifteen kilometres away.

What I do well, I've found, is get my sights on quickly and from maximum weapon range. I checked the distance and saw I was closing, so I cut my speed right down and let rip. Straight away I got the feedback that told me I was on target. But Ferdys turn good too and he spun around and must've cut in his injectors, 'cos he was lighting out fast and I thought I'd seen the last of him.

I pulled round in a wide arc on the edge of the furball, looking for someone else to pick on as soon as my laser was ready. There were a couple of flashes that let me know some ships were gone already, but I hadn't time to see who was left or even to count the traces on my scope. A Sidewinder screamed past me with a missile trailing it, I couldn't see who it was or what side it was on, but I hoped the ship wasn't one of ours as I'd noticed at least one missile boat in our line-up, and anyway Pythons can carry a couple. I didn't hear any ECM, but with a real quick glance on the scope I saw there were at least two blue-white traces on it, and that often means both sides have fired missiles and they're waiting to see who chickens out first and ECMs his own along with the other guy's. That was something I remembered from training, anyway.

I found myself with a Moray Star Boat in my sights – a

pretty ship, but I hadn't time to sit there and admire. I was still busy trying to score my first kill on this trip, 'cos scaring off the Fer-de-Lance didn't count, and it might even be back –

"Watch your tail, *Get An Honest Job*!" screamed the commset, just as a red glare filled my screen. I watched both my shields being scrubbed away, the sure sign you're being hit halfway down where they overlap. I broke, just in time to see a ship screaming in from the side –

And collide with the Ferdy that was a hundred metres off my six and following my every move.

* * *

When there's violent death all around, you just have to hope it's someone else's.

I didn't even see what the ship was that hit the Fer-de-lance behind me, still less whose it was. For a moment I was terrified it was Maussa's, if only because she was the only other pilot in our line-up who I even knew. But there wasn't even time to worry about that. The Moray Star Boat was pulling up hard and was happily going to play chicken with me, and my shields weren't up to it right at the minute thanks to the hits I'd just taken from the Ferdy. I pulled my stick into the corner and gave the yaw pedal a boot as well, wrenching my own guts sideways as I did it but willing to do anything other than run straight and level, which would have been a suicide note right then.

Thankfully someone else teased the Star Boat off my tail and I was left a few precious seconds to recover. In the fight so far, I'd fired once, nearly fired a second time, nearly been killed and been bailed out by a miracle that had cost someone else their life. It was a big leap up from the first trip out, just the daycycle before.

Experience is a wonderful thing as long as you live long enough to profit from it. When we Witched into Maesin I had my battle plan pretty well thought out, which is great if you can actually stick to it and, even when you can't, better than just flying in there and waiting for the other side to dictate to you. Our freighter this time was a Boa 2, also called a Boa Class Cruiser, and a superb piece of kit it is too. She's faster than a Python, more cargo space, has the power for military-spec shields and more hardpoints than you know what to do with. I flew close in to admire her, and just maybe to check out her pylons in case the boss saw fit to drop a mine in mid-battle.

Seeing nothing but missiles, I breathed a little easier. You like to think that no trader's going to drop a mine and accidentally forget that some of his escorts can't run away in time with no injectors, but I'd be astonished to see proof that it had never happened.

One after another we dropped into the wormhole behind the 2, with Maesin just a few hours away in Witch-space. There's a whole lot of weirdness to see in there, but it's always the same weirdness and after the first few times you've pretty much lost interest. You don't need to do any piloting either; you can't do anything except drop out of the other end of the tunnel, and even your arrival velocity is fixed, although that can change more or less straight away.

And if it doesn't change more or less straight away when your scope is full of red traces and someone's saying "That's the ship Eeci O'Fannonsdottir hired. Take it!" there's something wrong with you.

Like anything else, you learn to deal with assassination hits. They're there to do a job and they figure on delivering value for the money they charge, which is a lot, but they don't much like seeing their numbers go down and nothing to show for it. I was already hitting the taps as we came out of the tunnel and I spotted the bunch of hostiles, just about my ideal range. I locked onto one, knowing that in the first case they'd be trying to take down the Boa Class Cruiser they'd been hired for, and burned him in one economical burst. I was front-on to them at just about fifteen k's, and a Sidewinder's a tough mark at that distance – and when the return fire started getting too close for comfort, I pulled around edge-on to them, giving them an even smaller target, and whipped along straight for a few seconds before turning back round and rolling a quarter-turn to my right.

Soon as my laser cooled, I opened up on another of them. They were getting fire coming in from the other flank too and they didn't like it much, and this time, when they started getting my range again, I was all ready to pull the same move again, only in a different direction this time. That's where the quarter-roll came in. I'd thought this one through and practised it, and it was working a treat.

The other part I'd thought through was that when the assassins cut and run, I didn't even bother trying to follow them. I let my laser cool and my shields top off, closing back in on the Boa Class Cruiser and waiting for the next hit.

Well, the scum and villainy came and gave it a shot, but it was another of those missions where all the grief's happening to someone else. I made good and sure that no-one got much within that magic fifteen kilometres – not until I was ready to close the range and slice 'em up. It worked like a treat, again and again. One way and another, I rolled into Maesin station with five more kills to my name and a huge sense of feeling good about myself.

I hit the bar with a celebration on my mind – not only was it not my turn in the barrel that day, but I'd greatly enjoyed cramming a bunch of evildoers in there, one after the other. I felt three metres tall and every millimetre of it swagger. It was a night for chugging a large dose of some seriously good liquor, marking out the hottest girl in there, and spiriting her out from under the noses of all the guys to show her the kind of a good time that only another girl knows how to hand out. And, with next to no modifications, that's how it worked out.

* * *

The same job that seemed really easy one day can seem impossible the next.

Whatever nice stories I might have been telling myself

about a triumphant homecoming to Qudira – and I sure felt like I'd earned the right one way or another – they didn't last too long once I got a look at the reality. Qudira system was really busy that day, not just the reception committee but another mob when we got a bit closer in, and I couldn't put a single one of them down. I kept giving it my best shot, and my best shot kept on being not good enough, and even when I scored a hit I either ran my laser into overheat before the goonie blew, or else I lost my lock, or else I had to take evasive action on my own account.

Some days are just like that, I learned later, but at the time it had me chewing lumps out of my steering yoke, convinced I'd just been lucky with the one kill I'd got the last time and I actually wasn't good for anything at all except to give my wingmates a liability to take care of. And the second bunch were really annoying, not just for me but for the rest of us, darting in to see if they could score some cheap shots before breaking off again, too many of 'em with injectors that they could tap to get out of range quicker than we could follow. Our freighter captain made encouraging noises, saying he was fine as long as we got the cargo down to the Coriolis station, but it sure didn't comfort me having to keep an eye open for that pack of rats for a good hour and a half, always just one side or the other of the twenty-five kilometre line where your targeting computer loses its lock and you can just see a metallic glitter in the darkness against the backdrop of stars to remind you that you're not getting any peace.

They finally hollered enough just as we were reaching the edge of the station aegis and could have counted on some Vipers if they cut up any more trouble. A few violet traces on the scope would have been welcome long before, but GalCop doesn't have much reach in a system like Qudira – they keep the few police ships they can sponsor close in to the station, and try to hang on to them while they can. Viper pilots, I don't mind admitting, are even more underpaid than we are in some systems, and it's right up to the limit in an every-man-for-himself hellhole like the system I was born in.

Which is why it felt good to breeze into Maesin system and making like the toughest, saltiest critter in all the Eight on the strength of having come in mob-handed, armed to the teeth, and kicked ass every which way down to the station. Sometimes you'll dock and hit the bar glad to be alive, and sometimes you'll feel like you deserve to lord it all over the lower lifeforms, meaning anyone who isn't a spacer laser-for-hire jockey like yourself.

My hot girl snuggled up to me a little extra-sympathetically round about the time the party was finally over – by which I mean our private one; outside our door it sounded like there were still a few that were whooping it up – and asked "Tough trip, lover?"

I grinned evilly. "Not for me it wasn't." I dare say it was a little tougher for the unlucky five who'd crossed my sights.

"You lose somebody, then? Sorry – I'm not sure I should be asking."

She was right as far as that went, and I asked, a little tetchily, "Well, why ask then? The answer's no, for what that's worth."

"I was afraid you were hurting, that's all. You... You were rough, you know."

And Eesti forgive me, but I gave her the asshole's answer to that one: "I didn't hear you complaining, sweets."

I was sorry for it soon enough, but again, it was another protocol thing. Most bar-girls aren't going to complain about spacers, not for anything short of wilful assault. She gave me a much more patient answer than I deserved at the time. "Well, no. You know what buttons to press and how to press them, and you could see and hear for yourself what that did to me. But I'm still sore right now, and I guess I wanted to know if there was a reason."

It was still taking too long for the remorse to kick in, which is why I carried right on being an asshole. "Well, I'm sorry," I said, in the tone that makes it code for "I'm not sorry at all and how dare you make a fuss," and added, "What's the matter, decided you're not into girls after all?"

I should've got smacked for that. I might be all kinds of bad news when I've got a beam laser in front of me, but I don't know that I'd stack up all that high in a straightforward slap-fight. Instead she rolled out of bed and picked up her clothes. The stuff they wear along to the spacers' bar doesn't take long to get out of, but it goes back on again just about as quickly. Maybe she was figuring I'd take my cue to realize I owed her a few kinder words that might have got her to stay until morning, but I was just too bloody-minded at the time.

"Just so you know," she said when she was dressed, "a lot of the guys I see through here really don't have much idea how to show a girl a good time. They just don't know what to do with what they and I have got, for all their talk. But they try, they have good manners, and not one of them was ever rough with me on purpose."

And… exit.

* * *

Another day, another bar, another gloom.

I didn't see a whole lot to celebrate when we hit Qudira system. Sure, I was alive and I might not have been, but that wasn't enough to me, not when I'd been telling myself all these lovely stories of how a golden age was going to come to my homeworld one day soon, and I'd be a part of the reason why. We'd had a rough time getting in, we were a couple short, and I had an uneasy feeling about one of them. I was just glad it wasn't Maussa who'd hit the Fer-de-lance on my tail, but it felt like someone who I didn't even know had rammed that pirate just to save me from getting burned, and I didn't feel worth it.

Maussa told it different, though. "Saw the whole thing as I was on my way over. It was the *Death or Glory*, don't know the pilot's name but I saw him the night before… that was before things got interrrrresting," she purred. "He was a hot shooterrrr, liked to practise on asterrroids and he rrreckoned he could blow one, then blow one of the boulders, then blow one of the splinters, all without thrrrottling back or overheating his laserrr. I guess he thought he could pull that on the Ferrrry and it must have had a shield upgrrrade."

I wanted to believe her, but: "You sure?"

"Surrre?" she laughed, her tail twitching a mite. "No-one's ever surrre. All I'm saying it what it looked like to me, take it for what it's worrrrth. And learrrn. We all have to take rrrisks, but you need to think it thrrrough and take the ones that give you the best chance. I like to get on someone's tail and take my time to make surrre they go down, but the moment someone's on my tail I get out of there like a scalded... well, you figurrre it out. But that's playing to my strengths. Yourrrs are probably different."

I sat down and thought it over, and turned in early. Despite what Maussa had said, it wasn't a night for hard liquor and soft arms, at least not for me. But at least I'd got back to Qudira in one piece, and if that wasn't the homecoming I'd hoped for, well, it was still a homecoming of sorts.

Maesin, on the other hand, was somewhere I was looking to get away from. Even by planet dawn I hadn't got around to thinking any of it was my fault, but the next trip out turned out to be a long one with several Witch-jumps in a row before we made our next station. That happens sometimes. Freighters can take on Quirium at a fuel station or a satellite, or they can even sun-skim for it, which I hate because our heat-shielding isn't up to their standard and never can be. You can get mighty hot deep in a star's atmosphere, watching the temperature rising to the point where you're going to burst if your freighter doesn't hurry up and open up a nice cool wormhole.

This time, at least, it was fuel stations all the way, with us keeping a watch out while they were pumping because you get plenty of goonies that far out and they're not above firing on a fuel station to try to blow whoever's inside it. But so far as that goes, we did okay at seeing the bad guys coming and we dealt with 'em capably.

Long-range missions like that are tiresome, leaving you with your rations needing to be completely restocked and your space pants tested to the limit of the manufacturer's claims, but at least you can't accuse the traders of cheaping you out. They're not making any money until they dock, so if it's one trip for them, why shouldn't it be one trip for you? So the reasoning goes.

Anyway, I had plenty of long hours to look at my reflection in my blank viewscreen, and sooner or later I guess my conscience must have finally awoken, and I looked at the smug little face in front of me and I said "You scumball".

Of course by then Maesin was a long way away and it was likely to be ages before I was headed that way again. Escorts wander all over the galaxy depending where the next trader is bound for. If you really wanted to pick and choose then I guess you could only accept missions that were taking you the right way, but it's bad business and bad manners; all the other spacers have to take whatever's up next and they expect you to do so as well.

At the end of it we'd fetched up at Diora, about as unremarkable and nondescript a place as you'd find anywhere. Middle-of-the-road government, middle-of-the-road tech, and an economy that was neither one thing nor the other. I guess if you're a typical Communist worker bee then it's as good a place as any, and if the entire Galactic network were to collapse then Diora could bumble along for centuries by itself, turning out just enough machine tools and so on to keep the food production up, but it's a dull old place and even the Coriolis station didn't have much excitement.

Not that I felt up for much excitement myself anyway. I checked out of the spacer-bar party before it really got started, spent some time in my own pit for a while before realizing I wasn't going to sleep, then went for a wander. There's very little going on in a Coriolis station on nightcycle, and I fetched up in the general R&R area by default. There was just one old freighter captain there, who looked up momentarily, realized I wasn't hooking, then gave me a friendly smile anyway while he carried on tinkering with something. Oh well. That looked about the only entertainment I was going to find right there.

* * *

There's one thing that will get everyone to drop their quarrels right away.

If you've ever even considered going into space, much less actually been there, you'll know what I mean. Thargoids. It's quite something to be going about your business in the middle of a dust-up and then see the trace appear on your scope, flashing red and green, and everyone, trader, escort, miner, pirate, smuggler, assassin or cop, suddenly stops whatever it was they were doing and takes up Bug-splatting at once.

It happened to me sooner than I liked – just a couple of hops out of Qudira, when I'd managed to score a couple of kills to settle my rookie nerves a little, but still while I was officially rated Harmless. There were just the two of us, me and another Sidewinder, escorting yet another of the nearly-broke Pythons that somehow keep the star trade open between them, and we were looking nervously at a much bigger group of ships, the usual mixed bag that might be an honest trader or might be anything but, and all of a sudden the scope goes wild and all of that other group are steering straight for this green flying saucer with their lasers lighting up the emptiness.

Unfortunately they didn't have the proper training, and they didn't know that if you hurt a Thargoid bad enough it start launching drones at you – it never runs away – so pretty soon we had the mother ship and four or five robot fighters on our hands, which is bad enough to begin with and worse if another saucer shows up.

Which was just what we got, moments after someone had just yelled to stop shooting the robots and take down the saucer, and then someone else bawled "Belay that! Another warship incoming! Shoot what you can!" because, of course, if you take down one mother ship then any other one nearby will take over the drones.

I didn't like my first taste of Thargoids one bit. They have this nasty turret laser that means they don't have to be aimed at you to shoot you, and the big ships are scary quick. The only thing you have going for you is the part about never running away, even when a smart combatant would be breaking off to let their shields recharge. That meant, when enough of us hit it hard enough all at once, it gave this weird yelp of random words just as it blew, and once we had both the warships destroyed the robots just hung there in space twirling aimlessly. GalCop are just as pleased to see them blown, even so, so I scored myself a cheesy kill and a small bounty.

If you want to know what kind of nonsense a Thargoid screeches when it blows, by the way, ask any library computer. Spacers log the choicer ones for everyone else's amusement.

The thing is, I can understand space bugs being monsters, because that's how they're made. It's humans' inhumanity to each other that I can't get my head around – especially when I'm the one that's doing it.

I wandered over to see what the old freighter captain was up to, or at any rate near enough that he could shoo me away if he felt like it, and I'd understand if he did. He was a stocky kinda guy, not fat the way Fat Hannah was back on Qudira but way bulkier than any of my menfolks had been back on the farm and huge next to the singleship guys, who're all young and fit. There was a little grey in his hair, not enough to make him really old, and a beard that he kept trimmed all round, and he was dressed for comfort rather than glamour.

"Hi," I said. "Mind if I watch?"

He had a datapad in front of him and something sealed in a clear box, just a little gizmo the size of my top thumb joint, that was wired to a transceiver chip. "Sure," he said, tapping away at the datapad. "You can listen too in a moment, if you like."

"What's that you've got?" I asked, peering at it cluelessly.

"An antique. It's from the old Homeworld, if the dealer I got it off was telling the truth, which makes it... I don't know how many centuries old. Memory chip. There's music on it, once I get the decoder set up."

I listened while the datapad started to play whatever was on the old chip, and it was like no music I ever heard. I don't even know what it was being played on – I mean, apart from the datapad's playback program, which is pretty smart. It started out solemn, not sad but dignified, and then just as I was getting to like the tune it broke off into something else altogether, something that started off kinda joyful and light-hearted and then seemed to get carried away with itself. But then just as that second tune was becoming what you'd call frantic, back came the first one, and it seemed to say "Calm down. Stop this. Don't you remember where we began?" and it seemed to let the second tune, the frantic one, set the pace to begin with, but it took over, and said "Now at my speed," and it took right over, sonorous and grand, and it seemed to tear my insides right out of me.

"Who in all the world made that up, and what was it?" I asked the old freighter captain.

He smiled. "I'll never know. The best antiquarians I've found aren't even sure of the alphabet on this thing. There's just one word of speech they've found on the chip, sounds like 'Tanhoyzer', and no-one knows what that means either, or even if it's anything to do with the music."

I sat there in silence feeling the music let go of my soul at last. Eventually I said, "Why are people mean to each other?"

* * *

Sometimes you really believe humanity's going to make it.

When we got hit by the Thargoids and for just a few

minutes everyone human – or even just on good terms with humans – stopped what they were doing and all helped each other deal with the most inhuman menace in the galaxy, it seemed like there was an actual sense of hope that you could feel running right through that moment. And when the last of the Bugs went down, everyone sorted themselves out peacefully, the traders carried on in or out of the system and anyone who wasn't there with honest intentions just took themselves out of the spacelanes, even if it was only just until next time.

That gave me a lift at the time, and when I took off with my next trader I wasn't quite so on edge any more. I was lucky enough to get a few trips that were light on pirates and I managed to easy myself into the escort's routine. It wasn't always that way. Sometimes there'd be more than we could handle easily, and from time to time one of the escorts would go down, but I learned to accept that as part of the deal and to celebrate every trip where it wasn't my turn in the barrel.

And I'm not quite sure how that led me to Diora station, awake long after sack time, and listening to antique music with a trader who could've had kids of his own that were older than me.

He listened politely when I asked that question about people being mean to each other, and he didn't answer straightaway. Instead he called over the bartender, a fresh-faced youngster in Party drab, and got him to fetch over a clean glass, which he dirtied with a couple of fingers of something honey-coloured he had in a crystal flask that looked like it cost high.

"Sip it," he suggested. "It deserves respect."

He wasn't far off the mark on that, either, and you need to bear in mind I was already a veteran of many a spacer party. They're the kind where you gargle it down pretty fast and take a sober pill either before or after you and your companion get jiggy, but you certainly take one before you ship out in the morning. But the stuff they sell there is usually aimed at kids who've grown up too fast and need to act older than they are, only their tastes haven't matured as much as they like to think they have. This – well, it would have been rude to gag on it, but I figured he'd called it right.

"Thanks. Marilee, *Get An Honest Job*."

"Commander Macrae, *The Whisky and the Music*," he replied, giving the flask a pat to suggest where part of his ship's name came from. "You've something on your mind, girl."

And he seemed like the kind of old-timer you end up spilling your guts to whether you meant it or not, so I started doing exactly that, beginning with the disastrous run I'd been on just a short time ago, where only Terek and I survived and both of us rolled into a system we'd never been heading for. Macrae knew well enough what that meant:

"Failure. At least, that's what you'll have told yourself, no? And worse than failure – it's a taboo, isn't it? Never let your freighter get killed, no matter what?"

"Yes. Oh, yes," I said, meaning it more than the words could say. "Otherwise, what are we even for?"

He topped up his own glass with a suspicion more of the whisky; I wasn't ready yet. But I was ready to carry right on talking, and soon I'd got to the part where Terek ran out on me.

"So just when you need a bit of stability in your life, someone goes and yanks the rug from under you," said Macrae, "an' you feel you're worse off than when you started. Is that the way of it?"

"I wish it was," I said. "But I'm not done yet."

So I told him the rest of it, and he gave me a look that I thought was more sympathetic than I deserved. He didn't talk about what I'd just said, though. Instead he asked me a completely different question.

"Why do you do what you do – for a living, I mean?"

I shook my head. "I'm not always sure any more. I thought I knew."

"Let's phrase it another way, then," Macrae suggested. "How would you have answered – when you thought you knew?"

"Ohhh," I said, prevaricating over another sip of the

whisky, "several reasons. To save lives. Because I'm good at it. To help make the galaxy a little bit better. Because I don't know how to do anything else. Damn it, I was recruited as a kid, I had nothing else going for me, nothing and nowhere to go back to – and I'd shown an early talent for shooting things."

"Up to now I'm not hearing anything to make me throw my hands up in horror. But has something changed?"

Another headshake. "That's what I'm asking myself. It shouldn't have – but I'm not feeling the part about saving lives or making the galaxy better. Which just leaves me killing people for money, because I'm good at it, because I don't know how to do anything else."

He finished his shot of whisky, giving it the time it deserved, then gave me a look. "Someone who's good at killing people for money is, every once in a while, just the kind of help I need. I've a long trip coming, up to Ususor." If you don't have the Sector One map printed inside your eyelids, I should maybe mention that's just about the far side of the sector – measured the short way, at least. "I'll be needing an escort. It's just as easy for me if I don't have to find a new one every time."

* * *

Security isn't part of an escort's life.

The nearest you get to security is when you see the chance of some guaranteed pay-days coming up. They usually go one at a time and no-one expects differently. You sign up today, maybe, with a clunker of a Python with a hundred tons of food, ores and cloth on board, and you hop over to another system a day away by Witchdrive and sign off. Your pay's already banked so there's nothing to be done except to spend some of it on R&R and wait for your next customer. Tomorrow, perhaps it's a swanky Boa Clipper running a cargo contract from one side of the sector to the other, and it's your turn to escort him for a Jump or two. The day after, another Python maybe, or even an Anaconda with most of a cluster's valuables in its holds and a swarm of escorts all grinding along at what feels like five furlongs per fortnight. Whichever way, it's pick-up labour for a day or so, and the next day you hope to find a new employer.

It's rare enough for a Cobra to be hiring escorts in the first place, and rarer still for that to be a long-range mission. You can do the math for yourself. Even a stretched Cobra III might clear fourteen hundred credits on a full load of computers at the best possible mark-up; no-one's going to make a habit of spending the thick half of that on a pair of hired guns. So when you get a job offer from a Cobra commander, you figure he's making the money some other way, and any way you can think of, it's not going to be making for a quiet life.

He might have a hold-full of drugs, which you can sometimes pick up dirt cheap especially if the local manufacturers are trying to get the evidence out of the system as soon as possible before the cops close in. There are places – you have to ask around, but they can be found – where you can sell them as dear as computers or the best entertainment sets you can imagine, and if you manage that the profits are huge. I'd never knowingly escort a drug-runner, because I've never forgotten what Agent Elus told me back after the excitement at Fat Hannah's. On the other hand, escorts don't always get told what their freighter is carrying…

He might be shipping bullion, which they tell me is worth a fortune if you've built your rep up to the point where planetary governments are prepared to hire you to deliver a sizeable chunk of their federal reserves to the far side of the sector. Rewards are high because the economies of two systems are closely tied to the delivery and their entire banking system might wobble badly if it doesn't arrive.

Finally, there are people who need to get somewhere in a hurry, can't afford to wait for the regular liners, and don't have a ship of their own. Again, the higher they're willing to pay, the more is hanging on their safe and prompt arrival. And if it comes to that, a trader who's shipping bullion can perfectly well have a cabin or two set aside for executive transport into the bargain. The fuel's already paid for, and the extra pay's a very nice bonus.

All of these have the same thing in common: an excellent chance that someone will turn up to try to make a profit off your endeavours. High-value cargo draws pirates like flies to the southern end of a northbound bull, and desperate passengers usually have someone who's keen to see to it that they don't arrive on schedule. So the more escorts your trader can afford, the more likely it is that he does need them.

Of course I didn't understand any of this back when I was starting out, though there were some lectures during training, which I did my best to keep up with. What you don't grasp at that stage you gradually pick up as you become older and wiser. Or else you don't learn to spot when a contract is likely to be hotter than a Viper's drive, and you get surprised when the trouble starts.

So on the one hand I was more than eager to book myself in for a long trip and a series of pay-offs, and on the other I was burning with curiosity to know how Macrae was able to afford it. The most I was entitled to know, though, was how he stood with the law. He gave me a smile that I couldn't quite be sure I was reading right.

"Here's the offer," he said. "I'll undertake to stop at least once every forty-eight hours, and you're rehired and repaid every time we launch at three hundred and seventy-five credits per launch. I may stop more often, the same deal, though it's my call whether we have time for a layover. Don't fash, I know your crew accommodation's not so grand as mine and I'll see you get enough time station-side. I'll not sun-skim unless it's an emergency.

"When we dock, your time's your own until half an hour before launch, and you'll be there promptly. But you're cordially invited to dine at the captain's table should you so wish – and mebbe that'll give us time to talk over what bothers you.

"Now, how you dress aboard your Sidewinder's your own affair, likewise in the spacers' bar, but if you're out in public you'll wear a Macrae uniform. Get to the tailor's first thing, they'll run it up for you on my ticket. All agreed?"

And, just like that, he'd taken charge so naturally it never occurred to me to disagree. His datapad and mine chattered to each other for a moment, and my thumbprinted contract transferred to his at the same time as his uniform specs and credit for payment arrived on mine.

*   *   *

Other folks' customs are always strange.

Where the strangeness mainly comes in is that you grow up thinking the way you did things in your house was the way everyone did them, everywhere, and this turns out not to be true even when you travel as short a distance as will take you to the spaceport, never mind another planet. Travel broadens the mind, they say.

The most commonplace things can be the weirdest to get used to. Top of the list would be how other people dress, and how they sit down to eat. We didn't wear anything the least bit fancy on our farm, of course. Qudira makes cloth as well as food and liquor, and every once in a long while when the trader came around we'd get a new pair of pants and a shirt off his wagon, always with plenty of growing room and made more for warmth and long wear than comfort or looks. And that would be what we wore for a year or more, before we cast it off for someone younger or put it by until someone else needed it. There was at least one pair of pants we had that Grandpa wore when he was a youngster, and every one of the menfolks that came after him, in order of age; and you can believe that everything got mended until there was more patches than cloth, until all you could do was throw it in the rag-bag to go for patches or quilting on its own account.

We never went what you'd call real hungry, not on a farm, but we didn't waste food, or eat anything fancy that could get sold or traded for something we needed. And I ain't saying we ate like animals either, but we hadn't much by way of eating irons and as long as no-one grossed anyone else out then nobody pointed fingers.

They schooled some of that out of us in training. There's kind of a standard set of table manners and tableware that you'll see on any GalCop station, and it's understood that this will be polite enough for everyday use no matter who you set down with. It took a while for some of us to get to grips with it, especially when you figure some like me never had had their own knife and fork to themselves. We learned that some places they eat with fingers, some with sticks, some with a fork or a spoon or similar, and we learned how to manage every which way.

But back to clothes for a bit, 'cos I about fell right down when I saw what the Macrae uniform looked like. I'd seen girls in skirts and so on, even tried one on myself one time, but you better believe no-one dresses like that on a singleship. I explained about the space pants before – well, they're a necessity, believe me, and a skirt instead just would not work. Still, Macrae had said it was something to wear in front of folks, not at work or even in the spacers' bar, so I guessed I could live with it.

The tailor quickly ran up a new skirt to my measurements. It fell in folds and was made of some kind of stiffish cloth with a fancy design in black and white strands worked across and down on a base that was mainly a kind of blue-green. I'd not seen that kind of pattern before. There was a plain white blouse and a short black jacket to go with it, as well as flat black shoes and - which made me blink – a sash and a hat of the same stuff as the skirt. They very kindly gave me a holo to show how it all went on, complete with animation for those who'd not been brought up to such fancy dress.

However, I had a captain's table to dine at – and they'd mentioned this in training too, as something that wasn't likely to come up but might; it was about as high an honour as a trader could offer his hired help, and though Macrae had spoken as though it was purely something I could take or leave as I chose, I didn't think I ought to be too quick to turn it down. We'd had a quiet run up to Usralaat by way of Esgerean and Oresle, and when Macrae called a halt I was more than ready.

Besides, I was hoping to ask him something.

I wasn't prepared, quite, for the surprise I got when I saw that the boss dressed just as fancy as the hired help. It was unusual for me to see a man in a skirt – but I was soon to learn that wasn't the right word – and otherwise almost a copy of what I was wearing myself, although with an altogether more masculine cut to it and with some bits of silverware that mine didn't have. He was waiting near the bar in the commanders' lounge, but with a table set for two near at hand. I took one glance and realized I hadn't a clue what half the metal and glass was for, and I about bolted then and there.

Macrae, though, gave me a smile and even a fractional bow, which was more formal manners than I was used to, and signed for one of the waiters to seat me before him. There was something slightly sparkling in a glass already waiting for me, and I couldn't help smiling. "Bima water? Here?"

"Your registration gave Qudira as your homeworld," said Macrae, "and Bima water makes a perfectly good aperitif when it's suitably served. I hope it's agreeable."

"So do I," I said, "but I'm hardly an authority. I used to get given the tiniest spoonful when Grandpa made a batch. I think that was to discourage me from sneaking a drop for myself."

Macrae laughed, and gave the waiter a nod to start serving dinner.

*   *   *

Some kinds of weirdness are easier to deal with than others.

Nearly all escorts that I run across in the spacers' bar, and nearly all the traders I sign up with, are human, and most of those that aren't are close enough to count. Some are taller, shorter, funny coloured or maybe a bit bonier than you're used to, but you get used to that easier than you might think. Even cats aren't too strange, once you get used to the idea that they can walk upright, talk, and use tools and weapons. But every once in a while you run across something insectoid, or maybe something whose near ancestor was a for-real lobster, and then you have to be real careful about how you react, because some of them can be really touchy if you even look at them funny.

Wearing this strange formal outfit and sat across the table from a man wearing the men's version of the same – including a rather larger sash draped over his shoulder, and an actual knife tucked into the top of one of his socks – was peculiar all right, but I was enjoying myself far too much to mind. It was very, very different from the kind of R&R I was used to, which tended to follow the same formula: Party wildly, drinking too much and laughing a lot, for a few hours, then have energetic sex with the lucky stranger of your choice, then crash out for six to eight hours and take a pill to sober up when you wake up if you didn't do it before. Granted that usually defuses all the tensions of the day pretty effectively, but the change in routine was… welcome.

"You said something about the Homeworld the other night when I met you," I asked him over the main course. "You said the music you were playing came from there, or so the dealer said. Was there ever a real Homeworld?"

"So they say," Macrae said, "in which context, 'they' means 'one or more people at random from the general population, who don't necessarily know any better than you or I', of course. Some folks give the notion more head-space than others. Mine, for instance, are firmly convinced of it – and that they've kept the dress and customs of our ancestors intact throughout the centuries.

"I'm from Gerete, by the way. We're passing near the place on our way up to Ususor, but I'll not be making a social call as we go."

I looked up the system on my datapad. "Here we are. Gerete – several governments, not a unified world, but well up the tech tree."

"Aye, as good as it gets for a balkanised world in this sector," Macrae agreed. "We'd have a better police presence in the system if we'd all haul together, but there are other considerations apart from space police. We've a way of life and traditions to keep, and our parliament's keener on keeping that than havering on about a world government."

"If they ever actually get around to talking about it, that puts them a long way ahead of my planet, at any rate. Also, you know, even realizing that you live on a 'planet' or that there are any others anywhere."

Macrae took a forkful of his Usralaatian ragout, and I took some of mine, before he answered. "Indeed. Places like Qudira are the reason why I do what I do."

"Shipping valuable cargoes into places that badly need it? It's the same with me, I guess. I'll take what pays, but I want to think I'm making a difference too."

He topped up both our drinks, which weren't Bima water any more – a little touch of that, even skilfully blended by an expert barman, will last you a long while – but a local wine that had a little less kick than what they serve in the spacers' bar while being altogether more enjoyable if you had something in mind beyond getting wrecked as soon as possible. "Only, you had begun to suggest that your confidence was feeling a little dented, maybe?"

"I'd have to say yes to that," I said, sipping the wine as daintily as I could remember; the clothes seemed to warrant it. "Losing a freighter hurt – but if I'm to be selfish about it, that isn't the whole problem by any means."

There was a lengthy wait between the courses, which apparently went with fine dining and was punctuated with a small shot of some fruit spirit over crushed ice. I was, a little to my surprise, starting to feel it, while Macrae might as well have been drinking water to look at him. "Your young man running out on you?"

"Yes. That didn't help. I was feeling like I needed a little stability for once. It doesn't go with the job, of course. And I felt I'd gone a long way out on a limb by even admitting it – and to be honest, it's not boys that I usually feel that way about anyway."

Macrae nodded. "So that's you feeling doubly vulnerable, then; which makes the slap twice as hard when it comes."

"Yes. Poor me," I said bitterly. "I'm sorry, I'm not being a good dinner companion, and you've really worked hard on treating me. Spacer girls don't eat like this very often."

Something made me giggle, and Macrae's lift of the eyebrow seemed to say that I should go on, so I started telling a story I'd heard in the bar one time, about a rich older man who takes a young girl out for dinner, and she orders every expensive thing on the menu…

"until eventually he said to her, 'My goodness, does your mother feed you like this?', and she replied, 'No, but then my mother's not hoping to…' "

And then some instinct warned me to shut my mouth before I implied something very rude indeed about my host.

Macrae smiled. "Here comes the dessert now."

* * *

Being wined and dined is wonderful.

If I'd been asked to describe my idea of a luxury dinner with a perfect host, I couldn't even have imagined Macrae's idea of dining at the Captain's table. He put me completely at my ease over using the fancy silverware, he'd chosen the kind of dishes that weren't too rich for an untutored spacer girl's stomach but were exotic enough to be a real treat, he'd even hand-picked the wines and other liquor glass by glass to balance everything out perfectly, and right at the finish there was another shot – or "dram" as Macrae was calling it by now – of the glorious whisky he'd introduced me to a few nights before to go with the tiny plate of dainties that finished off the dessert.

By this time I was reluctant to kill the mood, but there were still things I guess I needed to talk out, and Macrae's ear was the most sympathetic I'd ever encountered. I glossed over the business with Terek for the time being and moved on to my Maesin bar-girl –

"and what makes it worse, I guess, is that I didn't even learn her name. Macrae, I'm not like that! What could I ever have been thinking of?"

He was giving his whisky the attention it deserved – which was a great deal, since by now he'd told me it was a good deal older than I was – but he was listening to me for all that, and only a slight burr in his voice that hadn't been there three hours previously let me know he'd matched me maybe two drinks for one. "Lassie, people don't always act according to the best they ken, and people who're hurting are more inclined than most tae stumble. Ye were feeling that the universe had kicked ye in the teeth, so ye go lookin' for someone else tae hand it on till."

"I really wish I hadn't, though," I said, barely doing more than taste a drop of my whisky since I was feeling every single spoonful by now. "There's this kind of – I don't know what you'd call it exactly; 'fan club' doesn't do it justice – maybe 'support network' is more the thing. Young women – older than me mostly, but still – looking to… I don't know what's stronger, whether they're drawn to what they see as the glamour and the romance, or they just feel that we've got the most dangerous life in the galaxy and it won't hurt them to give a doomed young spacer a pity-date."

I didn't say "date", exactly, and for a moment I wondered if I'd either alarmed the other diners or shocked my gentlemanly host, but he didn't so much as flicker. "And do you find that helps – having a guaranteed date in every port?" Which, by the way, he didn't say "date" either, but he said the word easily and as if it were the most appropriate and useful way to say what needed to be said.

"I suppose it does, really. 'Eat and drink, for tomorrow it may be your turn in the barrel,' someone once told me. I'm always glad of the chance to wind down – and until recently, I'd have always said I was grateful for it, too."

"Well, then. Suppose ye go back tae bein' grateful and actin' accordingly," Macrae suggested. "Ye cannae turn back time nor undo a hurt once done – nor e'en be sure when next ye'll be in Maesin system to make your apologies. Pay it forward if ye cannae pay it back; there'll be nae want o' chances, ye can be sure."

I took a deep breath and let his words sink in, far kinder than I'd been feeling I deserved. "You're a wise man, Commander Macrae, and thank you for an amazing dinner."

"My pleasure. Should I escort you back to your stateroom?"

I laughed at his description of a spacers' clean, comfortable but above all basic accommodation. "May I ask another favour first? I'd really like to hear that music again – do you have your music box along?"

"I do not," he said, "but ye're welcome tae come and hear it, if it's no' too late."

At another time and place, that might have been my way of inviting a man to put the moves on me, but I had a clear sense that, for whatever reason, Macrae didn't want to. Which was funny in a way, because by now I was feeling that I wouldn't mind one bit if he did, although I'd drunk enough that I'd need to sober up if we were going to have any fun. At any rate, he didn't so much as look as if he was going to try anything, instead just letting me into his quarters and showing me to a sofa. "Coffee? Brandy? Both?"

So I also got my first taste of another treat I'd never imagined back on Qudira – a glass of hot, sweet, brandy-laced coffee with a thick layer of cream floating on it. "Another Homeworld traditional, so they say. Ye can also make it with whisky, but I don't have any along that I'd insult by pouring it into coffee. It'd be delectable, no doubt, but there are standards."

Delectable was not a word I used much, but Macrae had the right of it and no mistake. He fiddled with the music box and his datapad, and soon the sweet music began to wash over me again. I was lost for words. The music seemed to make me happy and sad at the same time, if that makes any sense, and I shook my head gently in wonder. "Macrae? Does the music tell you stories?" I murmured.

"Ah. Something that unites humans on all worlds – stories in music, like pictures in a living fire," he murmured, "and no two people see or hear the same. Mostly it says just the one thing, Marilee: what's been lost and forgotten since we left our home?"

* * *

I don't make a habit of waking up in strange beds.

That meant I gave a bit of a jump when I didn't realize where I was for the first few seconds – in a bed that was a little more comfortable that what they have in the spacer cabins, although those aren't too bad. You need to remember that what I grew up with was straw covered with ticking covered with a sheet that made no promise not to be scratchy, and even a spacer bed is a big step up from that.

As I say, I gave a bit of a jump while I tried to put last night's events back in order, and guessed on thinking it over that Macrae and I probably had slept apart, and just slept at that. I've enough experience of waking up after an energetic bedtime that I can tell when nothing's happened. Even so, I was well aware that I wasn't wearing what I'd been wearing the previous night, and someone had stripped me down to my underwear – for which, again, you can probably guess the contrast with what I grew up with.

Well, no need to panic. What I was wearing wouldn't pass in polite company even if it wouldn't technically break most

75

indecency laws, and I looked about in vain for my Macrae uniform before spotting a set of coveralls that looked about the right size for me. I slipped out of bed to put them on, aware of having a head that was a lot less thick than it had any right to be even if I could do with rehydrating…

- And there was a glass of water and a soluble rehydration pill on the bedside table.

Someone had plainly been the soul of consideration after I'd checked out of the previous night's party. I could hear faint sounds of movement on the other side of the door, and guessed it was time to make myself known.

"Morning!" said Macrae, looking up from a hearty breakfast that told me he must have the constitution of a bull. "The maid said your uniform would be ready by…" he checked the time on his datapad… "about fifteen minutes from now, but I thought you'd appreciate something a little less grand to wear when you went and got your gear."

I laughed. "You've heard of the 'walk of shame', then?"

"Aye. You walk halfway across the station still in last night's party gear, and not a man or woman's going to credit that nothing happened no matter the story you tell them. Mind you, I've seen plenty on the dawn patrol that clearly didn't mind that much the night before.

"To business. We're headed up to Tiraor today. I'll be calling at any mines in the system but we'll just be making the one jump – a twenty-three hour haul, and we don't need to push ourselves any harder after the last one."

I was just as glad. From Oresle up to Usralaat is a good thirty-six hours in Witchspace, with precious little to do or see and always the slight apprehension that the Thargoids could drop you out somewhere between the stars, when you'd be sunk whether they got you or not. A run that was going to be just over one standard day was a lot more to my liking. Even with an hour or two visiting the Astromines, that left plenty of time for a layover at Tiraor station. "Thanks, boss."

"Well, enjoy it. We'll have another slog the next time,

ending up at Diedar – and don't, for the love of all you hold dear, mention the civil war when you're there. There will be an argument, and there will be a fight. Now, off with you once the maid's been. We're launching in forty-five minutes."

I filed the advice about the civil war away for future reference and hurried off once my perfectly-laundered uniform arrived. The overalls avoided some of the hoots and jeers I might have got in spacer territory, but I still had a few not-too-polite enquiries as to what I'd been up to. In all fairness, at another time they might even have been right.

Dead on the dot, I was launching right behind *The Whisky and the Music*, and formating a half-kilometre behind and to his right. From as close in as that, it was easy to see the Cobra was packing a lot of firepower, which went a long way to explaining why Macrae was happy to cross the sector with a single Sidewinder for company.

Communist systems are usually heavily policed. Back in the earlies, so they say, pirates saw them as easy pickings. Then they learned that the collective is more than willing to put out a flood of ships that, individually, are just about good enough, and in droves, can take down almost anything up to and including a major Thargoid incursion. That meant we could probably look forward to a peaceful trip, if a little heavy on the traffic.

Of course, "probably" isn't the same as a sure thing, which I should have known without being told, and which was reinforced when the commset passed on the radio traffic with the usual air of complete detachment: "That's *The Whisky and the Music*, right on schedule. Leave no-one alive, or we don't get paid."

I just had time to clock the variety of ships on offer when Macrae hit the injectors and pulled out at a speed I couldn't match. Some of the assassins could, though – a Fer-de-lance, an Asp and a couple of Cobra I's. That left me looking at three of my own who were looking to join in the fun as soon as they could catch up, although it made my life a little easier that they were more interested in catching up than in doing anything about me.

Which meant I could reduce the odds against me slightly, provided I could still remember how to shoot.

* * *

If you're shooting at my employer, don't turn your back on me.

I had a pair of Mambas and a Krait scurrying after the rest of the hit squad as fast as they could hustle, which was about as fast as I could and nowhere near an Asp or a Cobra on injectors. All I had to do was slot in behind them and decide which one to pick on first. I locked on to the Krait and gave him a sustained-fire shot from twelve kilometres to see how fast he could dodge. As it turned out, he couldn't dodge fast enough, though he had time enough to screech "You're making some powerful enemies, Hired Escort!" before blowing.

That got the attention of the other two, at any rate, and they had some battle-savvy between them, the two of them breaking in opposite directions and converging on me at a wide angle. I was already breaking on my own account, though. I knew very well that my laser would overheat before I put another one down and I didn't figure he would scare easily enough to be worthwhile.

I put *Get An Honest Job* through a series of tight turns to make it hard for them. They were good enough to get close and ping my shields a few times, which I didn't like much, and I was left wishing for a rear laser mount and a little more speed. Still, no sense wishing. I heard another scream come over the commset, and it was an encouraging one: "I'm taking heavy fire from the Cobra! Help!" – but that didn't help me right then.

Cool enough. I cut my speed, hard, and spun sharply, accelerating again as fast as my Sidewinder would wear it, sighting on one of the Mambas while trying not to give his wingman an easy shot. We were into a scrappy turning fight now, not the kind I like best but you take what you have and hope your reactions are better than the other guy's. My beam lit him up good and hot before he managed to break, cursing something about "an easy job for an Adder with a pulse laser, they said…". But I couldn't take the time to get back on his tail while I had the other one sliding into position to let his own laser do the talking.

That, sadly, is how it goes in a two-to-one. If they're smart enough and quick enough to pull away when the going is getting rough, their partner can usually buy them enough time to get their energy back and their laser cool, and then you have to start on them all over again. You can still win, but you have to be good enough to burn them in one shot and before they figure out which way to break. It was looking to me like I was better than either of these alone, but in for a long fight against the two of them.

Sometimes that's good enough, as you've taken two or three of the goonies off your freighter, and sometimes it isn't, depending on how much other bad stuff is going down. This time –

This time I was taken aback to see the Asp screaming towards me with his injectors at full aperture, which meant he went all the way from off the trace to in my face in just a handful of seconds. He was shedding more plasma than is really healthy for any ship, too. He just had time to yell "You're making some powerful enemies, Macrae!" before a red beam stabbed out of the darkness behind him, and he blew.

Just behind the red beam was another ship injecting nearly as fast as the Asp; *The Whisky and the Music*, alive, well, and breathing fire and slaughter. That was more than enough for the Mambas. They had a pragmatic approach to dying on the job, and they both lit out for the edge of the galaxy as fast as they could get there.

So yes, long story short, this time my freighter had more speed, more firepower, and by the looks of it more know-how than I had, and the only thing that stopped Macrae from running down both the goonies, I guess, was that we'd hit the system at the end of a long-ish Witchjump and he didn't want to waste any more fuel through his injectors. Or there may have been another reason: He wanted to keep a watch over his hired escort.

After all the excitement, a quiet tour of the system's Astromines was an anti-climax. There was no need for me to dock. I had the pleasure of admiring one of the ugliest artificial structures in the galaxy and thanking whatever fates had left me spending my days trying not to get blown up, instead of being shut inside a tiny little ship on an endless crawl around the asteroid belt breaking rocks for someone to scoop and take away, or spending twelve to fourteen hours a day feeding a solar smelter.

All told I'd been in the cockpit for a little over twenty-six hours solid by the time we docked at Tiraor station, and I was in desperate need of a freshen-up even if I'd managed to nap in Witchjump. Macrae gave me a bare half an hour to present myself for dinner, but fortunately the fancy clothes went on a lot easier the second time around – and I was starting to like the look and feel of them, at that.

Dinner was less elaborate than before, but still polite and formal. I felt at ease enough to venture a comment, though.

"Some fancy shooting out there, boss," I said, not too loudly in case he didn't want it overheard.

"Practice tells," he grinned. "And a Cobra III's not a bad battle-wagon when you buy her some performance upgrades."

"So I heard," I said. "Which ones do you have?"

A wink: "All of them".

* * *

If I don't retire to a farm, I want a Cobra Mk III.

I had a fair idea what they were like from the one I saw – and had a ride in – when I was training, and from the write-ups that you read when you're on a long Witchjump and you've slept all you're going to. Otherwise, I'd seen them from a few kilometres away outside a Coriolis station, or as a smudge at fifteen k's in my gunsight. I wasn't the kind to hang around the docking bay ship-spotting when there was a spacer bar to get to and a pair of space pants to get out of, for whichever reason.

We'd had another of Macrae's three-course dinners, but with less to drink and cooking that wasn't quite as fancy, and after I'd wheedled a little he was kind enough to take me down to the bay and show me The Whisky and the Music, inside and out. She packed the usual four missiles and also a serious laser in all four mountings – Lance & Ferman LF90s, the best that money can buy.

"They say side lasers are wicked hard to hit anything with," I said.

"They say right. So if you bother with them, you get lots and lots of practice. You can get software that'll remap your control yoke in the different views, but it's a mixed blessing – you're pulling on the yoke, and your sight picture's telling you one thing while your inner ear's telling you another."

His burr vanished completely when he was talking professionally, as you might say; but I was more interesting in giving the ship a good once-over than in listening to his verbal tics. Inside the crew cabin there were far more lights and buttons than I'd seen in the last Cobra III I'd taken a look around. "You'll know the theory, of course," he said. "Shield generators, energy replenishers, a whole bunch of aids for everything from navigation to target acquisition. I drew the line at a robot cat, though."

Everyone hears the stories of the space trader who got himself sponsored to a shiny new Cobra III with a hundred credits to build a business empire on, and the ship lives up to the stories in this respect at least: there's almost endless capacity for improvement built into the basic design, which is already fast and capacious compared to any other ship of remotely similar size. Sheer demand led some unsung genius to develop a cargo bay accessory that slots into place in a few hours, and just about every piece of fighting kit you can think of comes in a "Cobra III" version no matter what else it will or won't fit.

Macrae did have a passenger cabin on Whisky, and I had a strong suspicion that there was an occupant, but that's something you don't ask your employer about. When you buy yourself a taxi trip to the stars for what might be a few thousand credits, you buy privacy, and not even a hired escort gets to question that. I wasn't about to break protocol on that one even before Macrae invited me to sit in the pilot's seat, which I accepted eagerly while trying not to look as though I had been wondering when he was going to ask.

It's an entirely different experience from sitting in the seat of a Sidewinder. Macrae had forked out a few extra credits to get the seat re-upholstered and I could tell it must fit him like an expensive custom-made shoe. It was almost like a throne to me. They say that a Fer-de-lance's flight deck is even more opulent, but I can hardly imagine how. The sense of sheer power –

"Like to take it out for a spin?" Macrae suggested. I looked at him to see if he was joking, but he was already on the commset to request launch clearance. "Let the automatics take care of you until you get the call to clear the docking corridor. Then make sure you're pointing at plenty of empty space, and make your adjustments controlled and deliberate. Don't worry, all the weapons are on safety."

We emerged from the tunnel with Tiraor in mid-afternoon directly ahead of us. There was the usual crowd of traffic, an incoming trade convoy preparing to dock and a couple of People's Police craft – Rays, not Vipers – making sure no-one was entertaining anti-revolutionary sentiments. (I joke, but only just. They have a special branch of space police just for that.)

"Bring the speed steadily up to one hundred twenty five and come about nice and steady for the Witchpoint. Just the bearing, that is. We're not going so far out just now – we'll stay in the station aegis and just spot some traffic for now. Okay, now ease her up to maximum… and give those policemen a friendly wave."

The sense of sheer power was something I could feel, just as I'd guessed it would be. A Cobra III masses eight, maybe ten times what a Sidewinder does, but it can nearly match it in a fair race on either top speed or acceleration. So when I opened the throttle, I could absolutely sense the extra impulse through the soles of my feet and the seat of my pants, so to speak, and I glanced at the rear view to see the twin engine plumes flaring away behind far further and brighter than my Sidie's little drive ever did.

"Some other time we'll go and blast boulders," said Macrae. "Not today. Bring us around, acquire the station, and we'll request docking clearance. Then you can move over."

Yes. It was probably best if Macrae docked. I eased out of the pilot's seat into the co-pilot's – the flight controls aren't dualled – while remarking silently that modesty isn't strictly compatible with a pleated skirt and micro-gravity. But I managed as best I could, and of course Macrae wasn't so much as trying to sneak a peek.

* * *

You get used to keeping odd hours.

The one factor that no-one can do anything at all about is the length of time a Witchjump takes – which, spookily, is exactly as many hours as the square of the distance in light-years. Apparently this checks out to many decimal places, and no-one knows why given that both the standard hour and the standard year are completely arbitrary measurements based on how long it took the Homeworld to spin around once and go once around its sun. Sometimes you think that the universe was, after all, created by someone with a sense of humour.

This means that, give or take an hour or two, you don't have much say in what time you pitch up at a Coriolis station. Your freighter has a fixed amount of time inbound from the Witchpoint, unless he wants to detour via a factory or a Rock

Hermit or similar, so you can predict with fair accuracy how long your trip will take. This means, though, it can be any random time of local day when you dock. I've spoken as though we were always arriving just in time for an early evening freshen-up, some solid food, and then partying until station midnight and crashing out until dawn. Rather often it doesn't work out that way, and you look to turn in at some odd hour and then get yourself up and about eight hours later to see who's hiring – which someone generally is no matter what the hour on the clock.

This afternoon, for instance, I'd just got back from my Cobra flight with Macrae and he'd given me twelve hours until we needed to be off the station again. I didn't expect to find anyone much in the spacers' bar on my way through to my quarters – because the bar parties pretty much do run by local time, if only because that's when the station girls get off whatever their daytime duties were – and I wasn't especially looking, but I hadn't allowed for the effect of the Macrae uniform.

"You're in the wrong bar, lovie," said a girl a little older than me, who was hanging out with a small bunch of cronies. She didn't mean it nastily, though, so I just showed her my ident, at which she laughed.

"Sorry. You're dressed a little fancy for a spacer, that's all. I thought you must be new, or something."

"No, that's just my uniform," I said, ordering a fruit juice for myself and suggesting she might like something. "What my employer wants me to wear in public."

"Looks good on you, though. Very Lady-of-the-Something or other, like they have on Edzaon. Anyway, name's Keturah, *Haven't You Forgotten Something?* Pleased to meet you."

"Marilee, *Get An Honest Job.* Just get here?"

"Hour or two ago. Wait, you said you have an actual employer? Permanent escort?"

That's the dream ticket for most hired escorts – part of a team that tags around with one of the big freighters. Most of them prefer to hire and fire as they go, though, which meant I was sort of in-between.

"No, got a short-term contract though, just up to Ususor. One-way trip unless the boss decides different when he gets up there, but at least it's a few days' money, and the fancy clothes are just a fringe benefit."

"Benefit from where I'm sitting, too," said Keturah, and if that sounds a little blunt, well, spacers don't waste much time when they'll be blasting out in a matter of hours. She'd said quite plainly, "I like girls, you amongst them, and if you've a few hours to kill, why don't we enjoy ourselves?"

I grinned. "They're okay, but it's nearly time I was getting out of them."

"Alone or in company?" Keturah murmured, and the twinkle in my eye was answer enough.

Which is normally fine and dandy, and let's not misunderstand each other here, Keturah was a treat in her clothes or out of them – a little taller than me, darker skin that may or may not have been coloured for her, the typical spacer's build with just enough padding in the right places for those who like their girls to be girly – and she was more than eager for some private fun at the drop of a uniform hat. She liked me just half out of my uniform, which was the kind of uniform you can have all the fun you want while still wearing half of it, and I couldn't have asked for someone with less inhibitions or more idea what to do –

And, for whatever reason, we got to the point where I had to say "Keturah honey, it's not you, it's me," because however cleverly and patiently she was lighting my fuse, nothing was going bang.

Keturah had the good grace not to look hurt or disappointed, and I made the right noises about what she had been doing, which would probably have worked on any other girl and would definitely have worked on me ninety-nine times out of a hundred. I sighed and very carefully didn't push her away, because no-one deserves that unless they've behaved very badly.

We cuddled instead, which was very nice, and Keturah at least was thoroughly relaxed and happy, at least physically. I guess being with someone who turns out not to be into it after all would dent your confidence a bit, though I've always been lucky that way. Anyway, it was nice to have a warm body to hold for a bit, while we chatted aimlessly about nothing in particular – the little trivia of an escort's life, where we'd been, where we were going, the ships we liked to kid each other we'd own one day after we'd flown a thousand missions – and after a while I was feeling settled enough to doze off.

When my alarm went, Keturah wasn't there and my Macrae uniform was looking rumpled. An express laundry could fix one of those, at least.

* * *

Someone did mention the civil war.

I'd taken Macrae at his word on the subject, and when we arrived at Diedar, which was a full forty hours from Tiraor, I was ready for a nice quiet hour or so in the bar before dinner. We'd managed to arrive at local sunset, after all, which meant the evening freshen-up and dinner were happening at the right time of day. And at least I wasn't in uniform when the fight started.

Diedar's had a civil war dragging on for years, with GalCop doing its level best to make sure that no-one is smuggling in weapons from off-world and not always succeeding. The odd ton of rifles and ammunition does a very good job of helping to keep the war going, and even though there's supposed to be a single planetary government and votes for everyone, the northern and southern continents are still arguing over who should be heading it.

They both pay their taxes to GalCop, for what it's worth in terms of keeping the in-system police presence good and high, and I hear they even try to each spend more than the other on it. But if that gives you the impression of a nice civilised squabble, think again. The best you can say is that they don't have the ability to destroy each other's cities wholesale. They have to do it the time-honoured way, by marching in an army overland and using old-fashioned torches and blasting powder.

It was tragic reading for me, looking at how much this place had over Qudira – a stronger economy, better government, and much more tech – and shaking my head at how they were wasting it. Not even money and democracy put together can buy happiness, apparently, but the folks where I came from would have died to give it a try.

Well, I kept all these thoughts to myself, for I was fast getting the impression that when Commander Macrae dropped a hint it was a good idea to listen, but there's always some clot who didn't get the memo or thinks it would be fun to see how much you can stir the waters without anyone actually coming to blows. The answer, as far as I could tell, comes to: not at all.

Someone said something they shouldn't have said, someone said something back, before a minute was passed there was a full-scale row – because it turned out that some of the spacers waiting for jobs were Diedar locals, who only ply back and forth between the same few worlds in the one cluster, and as the law of Sod would have it there were some from both the continents – and in much less than two minutes the fists and boots were flying.

I'd just as soon have slipped out, if only I'd seen the trouble starting, but I wasn't used to the speed at which things can boil over in a high-pressure setting, which meant I missed my chance. I don't really have the height, weight and reach for that kind of set-to; I do my best fighting from fifteen kilometres away with a laser beam. But if you've even been a guest at that kind of party, you'll know that there are some people who'll just treat it as a free-for-all and clout whoever's nearest, expecting that they'll be doing the same and whoever manages to duck fastest, hit hardest, and be on their feet the longest, earns themselves bragging rights for the night.

The bar staff have seen this kind of thing often enough,

in any Coriolis station but in Diedar more than most, and their approach to dealing with the trouble was simple and direct: Give everyone five minutes to blow off steam, make sure the glassware is locked away, and then turn the sprinklers on. As I understand it, a nice fine mist is the best option for fire control, but for dampening down an excess of high spirits, they have the "deluge" setting which also has the added bonus of being just warm enough for the water to remain liquid.

At that point they announced that the facilities were closed for twelve hours, which left everyone slinking off to their own quarters with that night's party not even started, and me checking my face anxiously before I'd satisfied myself that there weren't going to be any permanent marks.

Macrae favoured me with a tolerant look when I arrived, still looking slightly damp and chastened although I'd taken extra care to ensure that my uniform, at least, was in tip-top order. I'd a slight mouse under one eye and a definite swelling at the corner of my mouth, even though I'd ducked fast enough to keep it from catching me squarely in the teeth. Still, the aperitifs and the amuses-bouches were ready, which as well as allowing me to enlarge my vocabulary further introduced me to a number of interesting and unusual foodstuffs from all over the local cluster. You hear about the famous dishes like shrew cutlets and edible wolves, but there are thousands of other delicacies that don't get mentioned in the guidebooks.

Do I need to mention that Macrae barely said a word about my dishevelled state? He murmured something about only being young once, then moved on to polite discussion about how I had enjoyed the run up from Tiraor and how I was feeling? I didn't feel he needed to know about Keturah, who'd not only got up before I did but shipped out as well, or about the lack of bang I'd managed to get with her, and that left me mumbling non-committal things until the main course arrived.

I was hoping he would have something of his own to talk about, and it turned out that he did. Macrae's not the kind of man to spend a formal dinner hunched over a datapad and neglecting his guest, but he had something to show me: a ship design like nothing I'd seen.

* * *

I decided I wasn't so sure about the Cobra after all.

The ship itself was a joy to look at – long and narrow, although those are relative terms, but Macrae directed his datapad to show a Sidewinder to the same scale for comparison. It had what looked like atmosphere planes at the rear end and I asked the obvious question.

"Aye," said Macrae, "it's re-entry capable, like a Moray Star Boat, although not a submersible!"

I laughed. The Moray's an incredible feat of engineering that started out as a sea craft that could take to the air, and then someone decided that since the pressure hull was already air-tight and there was plenty of room to squeeze in a ship's drive, they might as well give it the capability to go off-planet. It also packs Witchdrive and a few tons of cargo space and is a true go-anywhere, do-anything kind of ship – but most species don't need space-going submarines, and leave the orbit-to-ground tedium to transport shuttles.

"What sort of performance figures – or is that a trade secret?" I asked.

"Well, that's what we call 'commercial-in-confidence'," said Macrae, "but if you're not planning on spilling secrets to the competition, you might like to see these graphs."

Again he got the datapad to graph the stats for the Sidewinder next to this mystery ship. I was impressed. It had the Sidie on toast for acceleration and top speed, could stay with it in a turn at anything above a crawl, regenerated energy faster and could pack a shield booster as well as…

"Wait. This thing's got Witchdrive? It looks too small."

"It is too small. It's not intended for hyperspace."

"But," I tapped the datapad, "it's talking here about injectors…?"

"And what could be more useful?" Macrae asked. "Most designers don't bother with Quirium tankage for an in-system ship; fuel-injection came along well after Witchdrive, and it's always been thought of as an afterthought – and a handy way to give the hyper-ships a performance edge. But there's no technical reason not to design an escort vessel around Quirium tanks and no Witchdrive, and you can imagine the edge that's likely to give."

"I want one!" I said. "When can I trade in my Sidewinder?"

He gave a gentle laugh. "For now, I'm thinking it might be a little out of your price range. But if you'd like to give one a try… well, we might see what can be done. Here comes the *plat principal* now."

We tucked into some game bird – it was large enough for two, and Macrae said it was traditional for the gentleman to carve – while I wondered whether he was serious about seeing what could be done. He hadn't told me what the ship was called or who made it, or what his connection with it was, and I guessed I wasn't likely to get answers if I asked. But Macrae didn't intend to let the conversation lag.

"Not quite a genuine woodcock, but finding one of those can be a bit of a snipe hunt," he said, "and the chef here has a sure touch. Don't skimp on the braised vegetables, they're delicious as well as good for you. By the way and with your leave, I've some thoughts concerning your troubles with your young man."

I wasn't sure Terek ever had been my young man, exactly, and I had some fresh relationship woes I might have gone into, but it was kind of Macrae to have been thinking of me and I asked what he meant.

"I think it's that hired escort ethos that you've bought into," Macrae said. "Of course you're no' a navy, nor even a regular unit of any other kind – just a society of freelancers. What's your code of behaviour?"

"See that the freighter gets through, don't get yourself

killed, punish bad guys if you can…"

"And – stop me if I'm wrong – don't get attached to anyone or anything that might take your mind off your job," Macrae prompted.

"Yes. Seconds count in a fight, and if your mind is on someone or something else, you can get killed before you even realize it," I said. "It's all right to enjoy yourself while you're off duty, but what happens on station stays on station."

"Which, if I'm following all this correctly, means yon Terek was fixing to do you a favour. Ye daren't start thinking about each other, for you need to be thinking about yourself and your freighter – not necessarily in that order. So he concluded this before you did, and scrammed out o' there, not just for his sake but for yours."

I shrugged. "Deal's done now, isn't it? I mean, I guess you're right, but…" My voice tailed off inconclusively.

"Thing is," said Macrae, "I'm no' so sold on the idea that this escort ethos o' yours is actually right. In my experience – which is by no means all-encompassing, but still – human beings lookin' to stay alive for each other do at least as well as those just lookin' out for themselves."

"Well, in training," I said, "they had facts and figures to back it up."

"Which, no disrespect to your inborn smarts, ye'd have been ill-equipped to pick holes in," Macrae pointed out. "Still, this is just my gut feelin', if I'm honest, and it'd stand up better if I had some proper research to show you facts an' figures from. And it disnae detract from my main point, which is that your young man, by the lights you both live by, was likely enough thinkin' of your good when he left."

We hadn't been drinking very much yet, which left me wondering why Macrae's burr was becoming more pronounced. I sighed. "Perhaps it's just me… looking for somewhere to belong ever since my whole family died. Macrae… have you ever lost someone very close to you?"

He was silent for long enough that I wondered if I'd

overstepped the mark. "Aye, lassie. I have indeed."

* * *

Sometimes you just have to stumble, pick yourself up and carry on.

I was all set, I guess, to talk over how it was the day the family got wiped out, all except me, but I realized at once I'd touched a nerve that didn't ought to have been touched. Macrae took only a few seconds to recover, but it felt like I'd aged several years in the meantime. That was my cue to watch my mouth another time. It's not an escort's business to ask personal questions of the boss.

"We're getting maudlin," Macrae said – and I noticed his burr had vanished. "Let's look at our itinerary. We have… let's see… Riveis, Arexe, Xeean, and Edle – all about enough for one day. Ususor's only another four hours after Edle but the Xeean to Edle hop will take a full twenty-five hours, so we'll be ready for a stop-over and all the fresher when we get to Ususor. Watch out for strangers at Riveis."

I checked the map. "That's because of Atarza just next to it? The Anarchy system?"

"Yes. Point four of a light-year away – that's ten minutes in Witchspace, and the miscreants with fuel to burn if they have injectors. I'll not take us through Atarza system for all it would shave a number of hours off our run."

Extra distance racks up the time quickly on a Witchjump. Go four light-years followed by one, and you've taken seventeen hours in total, nearly all on the first jump. Do the five all in one go, and that's an extra eight hours. Of course, the extra jump could mean ringing the bell in a dangerous system, and even if you hyperspace away they can use your own wormhole to follow you. Even so: "I'm game for it if you are, sir. It's what I'm paid for."

"Thank you, but no. I know the schedule I'm running, and I can spare the time."

Of course, your trader can be setting out to minimise the risks all he can, and you can still find yourself meeting up with trouble no matter what. The warning about strangers at Riveis, for instance, was right on the money.

We dropped out of Witchspace just twenty-three hours out of Diedar to find that the miscreants, as Macrae so aptly called them, were loitering near the Witchpoint with intent to shake down strangers for cargo. They gave us some line about propping up the corrupt state, but the long and the short of it was, they were demanding money with menaces, which I well knew by now was something Macrae aimed to discourage as strongly as he could.

My part was limited to blowing up a single Gecko who Macrae didn't get first. The rest was clearly all in a day's work for my boss – and I'd not even seen him fire a missile yet, although he was carrying four of the best, the kind that have the anti-countermeasures built in and cost about twelve times as much as the regular torpedoes. I didn't see too many bumps in the road otherwise. All our waypoints were in nice orderly systems with efficient police forces, and even the assassins seemed to have fallen silent lately.

So the only unhappy part as far as I was concerned that I would very soon have to go back to earning a living, and no more formal dinners in fancy clothes with perfect gentlemen blessed with exquisite taste. Not that I ought to be complaining. It's almost unheard of for a trader to hob-nob with the hired help, even if the trader himself is one of these Cobra-and-a-hundred-credits legends that you hear about. The one exception to the general rule turning out to be a man like Macrae, instead of some slightly seedy older man who thought the phrase "hired escort" carried over into the twelve hours after arriving on-station, was a once-in-a-lifetime bonus. I didn't want it to end, but I supposed I didn't ought to be greedy.

What was surprising me, a little, was that I wasn't missing the spacer-bar parties as much as I would have expected. If you'd told me five days earlier "You've got a short-term contract coming up, pay's regular but you won't be frequenting the bars until the end of your hitch," I'd probably have said "Get bent, I'm having no trouble getting hired as it is and I'll stick to what I know and like." I just didn't do this whole business about getting dressed up for dinner and taking three hours over it and six different knives and forks – but I'd got to like it a lot.

Well, four more stopovers and then we'd be at Ususor and it would all be over – although I still wondered what Macrae had meant about giving a try-out to his mysterious new ship. If he was going there on a business venture and wanted someone to show off one of them to someone he was trying to sell them to – well, there are professional pilots for things like that, and they're not usually the ones who hire out as trade escorts.

Sufficient unto the day, I told myself – which was another one of Macrae's phrases that I'd picked up – and I followed him down to Riveis station.

Macrae continued issuing the dinner invitations, I continued attending them, and I carried on receiving an education at the same time as being fed and entertained, all of it at my employer's expense. That plus the general lack of serious nuisances on the way made it feel like an extended holiday, which was another thing I'd never really had before.

And we arrived far sooner than I liked in Ususor system, after a four-hour Witchjump from Edle, to find a reception committee waiting for us. I only carry the cheap scanner in my Sidewinder, not the one that scans the police bands – but even the cheap scanner will register hostile locks on you or your freighter perfectly well.

* * *

There's a level of force that no-one can beat.

It'll vary from person to person. Your greenhorn in his new Cobra III off to make a killing on his first twenty tons of food may find a single old Krait too much for him. At the other end of the scale, no one ship can fight off a thousand, even a hundred, even fifty, and for smaller numbers you still need an edge in speed or firepower – both, for choice.

The twelve ships coming in at us from all sides look as though they will be enough. They're coming in very fast. Do they all have injectors? I can't spare the time to check out all of them, I'm desperately trying to burn one of them in the time it takes to get from maximum range to in my face –

And I'm having to break off, even as I see that Macrae got one in the beam of his port laser and has blown him to dust and gas. But it was a long blast, and Macrae's surely got a hot laser there… and there are missiles heading for him. I hear the scream of his ECM and a couple of them burst, but not all.

Macrae's turned and is running. I'm following him, more scared than I've ever been, not just for me but for my freighter, I don't want to lose another one… and I realize as my stomach clenches and my heart thumps, it's not about my freighter. I'm actually crying here. I'm actually raging, "You murdering cowardly bastards! Twelve onto one?" It's not about my freighter, it's about Macrae.

"Kill them both," comes over the commset. I glance at my rear view. There's an Asp tailing me at barely five kilometres. It seems to loom over me and I feel as though I can see straight down the barrel of that huge gun mount they have at the front.

Murdering cowardly bastards!

Macrae's rear laser stabs out a moment before he gives his injectors a quick dab and pulls around. There are still two missiles on his tail and he's not even trying his ECM. They must have the hardened avionics. I jink to break the Asp's target acquisition, but I can't outrun it. I see its laser blast stab past me for an instant but its pilot has quick reflexes and cuts as soon as he sees he's not on target.

"Oh, you tak' the high road, and I'll tak' the low road, and I'll be in Scotland afore ye!" comes over the commset. The computer calmly reports that the message is from *The Whisky and the Music*, but who else would it be from?

Macrae launches one of his own hardheads. Then

another. He's acquired two missile locks in less time than it takes to say it, still ducking the ones on his own tail…

But two of the ships after us just break off, injectors flaring. They can get out of range and break the lock, and be back in half a minute. Half a minute's a long time in a space battle, but is it long enough?

"Boss! Inject away! Get those missiles off you!" I yell, and my commset calmly passes the message on. Then it reports one incoming: "Stop struggling, Marilee. It's over." The commset say it's from –

Haven't You Forgotten Something?!?

"Keturah!" I yell. I get my rear sights on the Asp long enough to get its ident. Headsmack. Why did I just assume she flew a Sidewinder like mine?

"Of course. I've come for you. Ironic, isn't it?"

It takes a moment for the double meaning to sink in. "Why, you…"

"Oh, don't. This isn't personal, it's just business. Now stop your wriggling and accept the inevitable. And thanks for the help."

I'm already ahead of her. I told her where we were going and it's thanks to me we're in this trap. There's still seven or eight ships converging on *The Whisky and the Music* and they aren't all missing, and no shields are going to stand that for ever.

"Stop dodging, Commander Macrae. Are you expecting someone to come and help you?" says a ship that is actually named *Nothing Personal, Just Business*. Macrae outright says "Ha ha ha ha ha…" – a commset won't pass on a laugh – and scratches another one of them with his rear laser. Just seven still after him, with the two that he missiled on their way back… but there are a lot of drive flames out there all of a sudden. Bystanders, or are they going to help – and which side? Whichever way it's going to happen, it needs to be quick. Macrae had to run straight to get that laser shot in, not for long but long enough to take a storm of hits.

I'm still afraid, but I'm enraged as well, and I cut

power, pull around, and set myself head-on at the Asp with my drive on maximum and my laser finding the mark. Let's both go together, Keturah!

"Tally-ho!"

"View halloo!"

"Reynard's broken cover!"

"Game's afoot!"

My commset is full of nonsense and I haven't a clue why. I don't have time to think about it. Keturah's laser is filling my viewscreen and my energy's burning away far too fast. But I don't care as long as she goes as well. I flapped my mouth and betrayed my boss and I don't deserve to survive this.

"Crazy little dirtbag!" comes over the commset as the Asp breaks at the last instant. She's shedding plasma, badly, but so am I.

"I say, play the white man, Stiffy. My bird, don't you know?"

"Oh, don't beef about it, Ginge. There's an Adder there that's more your mark."

I still haven't a clue what all this is about, but –

"Haud yer wheesht and pay attention to business!" sends *The Whisky and the Music*.

Then –

"Thanks for the assist," says *Haven't You Forgotten Something*. "Bye, Marilee." What –

"Warning. Hull breach."

* * *

Swotty Neville here.

The Macrae asked me if I could possibly set down a few words about how things went down at Ususor, for those of you who've been following what we found on the young lady's recording device, since obviously she – Well, if you've been reading up to now, you already know. Sorry.

It always seems to be me who pulls these assignments,

ever since Stiffy, Ginger, Nobby and I were boys together. I don't know whether it's because they genuinely have no idea how to tell a story, or are too bone bloody idle by half, or if it's just that I'm always half a second too slow to duck. Anyway –

But first I ought to give people their right names, I suppose. Not that Stiffy and the others would mind the least once they got to know you – and there's not an ounce of real snobbery in all of them put together – but, you know, while we're still officially strangers there are standards to keep up, what? So I'll carry on using the nicknames for now, but you should know that Stiffy Fitzalan is known to the world at large as Reginald, Earl of Arundel; Ginger Percy is actually Hugh, Earl of Northumberland; Nobby de la Pole is really Frederic, the Marquess of Suffolk; and all of this makes me Archibald Neville, Earl of Warwick. That's the introductions over with.

Now, the Macrae got word through to us that there was something in the wind. Exactly how he did it, I'm sure you'll understand I can't tell you, but believe you me, the Macrae's not one to drop a word idly. Equally, he's as good a man as you'll see when it comes to fighting his own battles, ever since – But that's his story to tell. Let's just say that firstly, if the Macrae's actually admitting he might be glad of a little assistance, you can take it as read that something monstrously unfair is being set up for him, and secondly, when this man asks for help, he doesn't need to ask us twice. Part of the reason is that he owns about a million acres up in the Highlands, all of it absolutely prime sporting land, and he's very liberal when it comes to letting a friend have the run of it in the Season, and of course he's the man to go to if you want to know what ticks in the whisky world. Mostly though, he's such a thundering good egg that no-one wants to be the man to tell him no.

Well, Ginger got hold of me, and I got hold of Stiffy and Nobby, and we warned a few other likely chaps to be on standby, turn and turn about as you might say just in case the Macrae got the time or the entry point a little off, only I'll not mention any of the others for now lest ill come of it, and we got the Purdeys greased up and ready for the off. Not to impugn your nous or anything, but I doubt you've seen a Purdey. They're all custom-built and never sold on to the general public, and the few that there are generally stay in-system although they're perfectly good enough for a quick hop over to Arazaes or Edle or Gerete. They're meant as sporting rigs, though, not long-distance space transports – but they also make first-class fighting ships when you take the buttons off the foils.

Without going into too much detail, let's just say that a Purdey is about as fast as you want, about as well-armed as you need bearing in mind that a missile is a blackguard's way to pot a bird, and – which is handy from time to time – rather hard to spot from just outside scanner range. And now I think I've probably told you enough to understand how it was we came to be lurking among a small clump of asteroids thirty-odd kilometres from the Witchpoint, watching for wormholes for all the world as if we were crouching in a stuffy hide on a damp morning waiting for the Monarch of the Glen to put in an appearance.

Of course you'll see any number of wormholes open up in any system, especially in Ususor where there's a ready market for those fancy electronics and a steady supply of whisky to ship out (but not the good stuff, and never believe anyone who tells you different). So we had to bide our time and watch for suspicious activity – such as ten to a dozen drive flames all edging around the Witchpoint as nonchalant as you like. Little did they know, we thought.

It doesn't take long to close the distance in a Purdey and start to teach a bunch of miscreants the reason why they should conduct themselves like gentlemen. Granted, by the time we were moving the Macrae already had a swarm of the blighters acting tiresome, but we set about evening up the odds as soon as we could, and it's no loose vainglory to say that we do it rather well. Of course we practise on "dangerous game" regularly, with the buttons on the foils of course – but that doesn't stop us knowing how to give a scoundrel the point when it needs to be done. Quite the reverse, let me assure you.

The Macrae bade us watch out for a Sidewinder, who was one of his party and likely to be out of her depth, and I must say we did the best we could, but she was sore beset by an Asp that had ought to be picking on someone her own size, and before we could get to her – and we saw her giving the Asp of her best, for all that – I'm afraid some scummish waghalter gave her a fearful searing with a laser. It would have been too much for her had her ship been in the best of order; and it wasn't.

* * *

Neville here again.

It's not good to be caught in a doomed ship with no escape capsule. The human body really is not designed to stand up to an exploding ship's drive, and even if it were, tolerably few of us turn out to be all that good at breathing vacuum, and less of us get much chance to practise.

It might surprise you to learn that there was any chance of survival at all. I'm afraid that ships will explode when their drive's containment field ruptures. There's nothing to be done about that until someone rewrites the laws of physics and comes up with an entirely new energy source for spaceships. For most of us it's enough to have something that will let you bat around a solar system pretty much indefinitely and not need refuelling – and which, if you have the right kind of hull and so on, will even let you land on a planet and take off again, or skim through a star's upper atmosphere – and it seems manifestly ungrateful to demand something that won't explode when you let it out of its bottle in too much of a tearing hurry.

What isn't beyond the wit of man, though, is to design a containment field in such a manner that, when a ship blows, there's a safe zone – roughly conical – that won't get torched by the hellish energies being loosed on the inoffensive vacuum of space. That's darned handy if you have an escape capsule and are just a half-second slow punching the eject button, and it also means you have a fool's hope if you don't.

You then move on to that business about learning to breathe vacuum, which of course is utterly imposs., and in fact your best hope – insofar as you actually have one, which you naturally don't in all but the most freakish set of circumstances – is to let your breath out in a controlled but above all rapid fashion before you rupture the one and only set of lungs you were issued with. That leaves you with a tiny amount of oxygen in your blood, although for the little that it's worth, the vacuum will keep the carbon dioxide levels in your lungs vanishingly small, so at least your nervous system isn't frantically signalling you to breathe when there's damn-all to breathe in. You'll black out very soon, of course, but you'll do so largely painlessly, although I for one don't care to make a habit of it.

Now you'll remember that I mentioned about practising on "dangerous game", and the most dangerous game you'll find, on or off-world, is a man whose training and armament is a match for your own. We're rather fond of space duelling in Ususor system – some more than others, admittedly – and while we do take care not to space each other carelessly, we do take account of the fact that accidents will happen.

When they do, you can either weep, wail and wring your hands, and then make manly statements at some poor devil's funeral, or you can move efficiently into action confident in the knowledge that you have prepared for every eventuality as best you can, and no-one needs to end up dead if everyone does his bit. That's what happened when *Get An Honest Job* blew up.

First of all Stiffy cried out "Rider fallen!", and Nobby called out "On it! Keep the miscreants busy," which of course we were all doing to the best of our ability and no small effect as it was. Now Nobby's Purdey was equipped, as was mine and Stiffy's and Ginger's, with the necessary accoutrements to rescue some poor soul who'd just been consigned to hard vacuum, always granted one or two minor considerations such as remembering not to hold her breath. The first one was an extra little sensory device that no-one much bothers with because no-one much needs or wants.

A human body's an inefficient radiator, what with the temperature being so low and all. Even so, it's perfectly possible for sophisticated electronics to pick up a human body's warmth at a range of a few kilometres, as long as you're not looking for it against the sun. Can't expect miracles, you know.

You then need a device not unlike those fuel scoops that a lot of merchants carry – and yet not entirely like, for all that. A cargo canister's very solid metal and can stand rough treatment, even if there's some poor devil of a slave inside it. Flesh and blood needs gentler handling.

You also need a pilot who can lock onto this warm body, make the best of his way to it, and get it safely scooped up in a single pass; if you miss the poor blighter you're at grave risk of passing him or her through your drive flame, which is odds-on to be immediately fatal.

Taken all in all and considering the astonishingly poor chances involved, you'll understand why most spacemen will cheerfully shell out the denarii for an escape capsule, even at slight risk of being scooped by the wrong side and sold for a slave after all or, if the opposition is feeling particularly bloody-minded, blown up while you're helpless. Since the ungodly on this occasion would surely have skewered any escape capsule fired from *The Whisky and the Music* or his escort, you can see why it wouldn't have helped much this time.

However, if you've once been fortunate enough to have had all of the above go pretty much according to the maker's instructions, and you've not succumbed to brain damage in the meantime, your chances are excellent if, while your rescuer's brothers-in-arms are dispatching the rest of the baddies to the region where the woodbine twineth, you yourself are being gently repressurised in, for choice, about two hundred hectopascals of best O_2.

All of which, I'm pleased to say – and apologies for the epistle, but this is indeed why they call me Swotty – happened.

* * *

I never expected to wake up in my own coffin.

No matter how I try, I can't make the memory come back – of the few seconds after my Sidewinder exploded, and I went tumbling into the void. Apparently I let my air go, and I must have been conscious for several seconds while I went hurtling head over heels at about the speed of my vanished ship. I may even have seen a gleaming black shape appear against the backdrop of stars, match velocities with me with impossible precision, and gather me into its belly. But my brain won't bring the image back for me. It's gone, like a dream that vanishes when you wake and you never recollect again.

So I can't swear that I ever even lost consciousness, but I didn't regain actual awareness until I was in this narrow compartment that was just big enough for a rather larger human being than me, with a gentle hissing in my ears that told me air was being brought in slowly and patiently.

"Don't be alarmed, Marilee," said a voice through a speaker. "You're in safe hands. Are you badly knocked about?"

"Macrae!" I gasped – not because I'd mistaken the voice for his, but because I needed to know how he was. The voice seemed to grasp what I meant, luckily.

"The Macrae is doing just fine, and you can save your sympathy for his opponents," the voice reassured me, "and I ask again, are you badly knocked about?"

"I – I don't think so," I said.

"Bleeding?"

"Can't feel any… let me check… no, I think I'm okay." If I was bleeding into my space pants, I couldn't find out until I had room to take them off; they're too bulky to make much of an examination through.

"All right, I'm going to take that as meaning you'll live for the next half an hour or so. Heading on down. There'll be a sedative coming through in a moment. Don't fight it, there's a love."

103

"Macrae!" I gasped again, and once again the voice seemed to know what I meant.

"He already knows you've been picked up – and it's all quiet out here now. I'll let him know you're doing all right and asking for him – now you just have a nice cosy nap."

I had no trouble doing as he said, which was certainly for the best – being carried along blindly in a tiny container while a ship makes a dash for the Coriolis station is probably something that's best slept through if you have the option. I don't know if he was a little heavy-handed with the sedative, but the next I knew was after I'd already been let out after the ship docked, and stretchered away to a clinic that was a step up from any medical facility I'd ever seen.

There was an instrument panel on a trolley next to my bed, with a whole set of sensors stuck to my body that were, I guess, communicating wirelessly with the panel. All the lights were green, which was reassuring.

And Macrae was sat in a chair next to my bed, completely unharmed and in the best spirits I'd ever seen him. He grinned. "Glad to see ye made it, lassie."

I held out my hand and he took it, and then I closed my eyes to try to keep the tears in, and didn't really succeed. "I'm sorry. This was my fault."

"How so?"

"Tiraor station," I stammered, "the last girl I slept with... I forgot to keep my mouth shut, I told her where we were going, I was in uniform... she was with the assassins and she must have known the Macrae colours if they've been after you. I'm sorry, I'm so sorry."

I felt a soft pad of cloth on my face. "Dinnae talk daft, child. It was nae fault of yours."

"It was!" I insisted. "It was a stupid mistake and it's not like I didn't know better, I shouldn't say anything to anyone about where my employer's going, all the more if they've got the whole time we're crossing the sector to set you up!"

"But that's what I wanted," Macrae said, and my eyes

blinked open. "Aye, ye heard me right. I couldn't count on yon rapscallions hearing it from you – but I left plenty other breadcrumbs as I was going. I knew well enough there'd be a trap laid for me, and what I was after was to lay another one of my own."

My eyes widened – and then, despite everything, I began to smile. "You scheming old…"

"Compliment accepted," said Macrae. "An' ye'll understand that I couldna let ye know what was going down?"

I nodded. It was obvious. What I didn't know, I couldn't betray by some unintended word or gesture – anything that might have stopped Macrae from turning the trapper into the trapped. But… my ship was gone, for all that. I gave a brave smile my best shot. "Is there any chance I'll get to find out what this was all for?"

"Aye, an excellent chance. First, though, I'll see to it that ye're a free agent. If ye but say the word, I'll spot ye a brand new Sidewinder to continue plyin' your trade in. Alternatively, I can make it a Cobra Mark One plus a few highly desirable extras – injectors, beam lasers, and some trading capital."

I blinked in astonishment. "That's… an outstandingly generous offer." Not the Cobra III of my dreams, but a viable trading vessel for all that.

"Alternatively," Macrae said, "an' it might entail a free ride in a ship we were discussing just the other day… I'm heading down to the planet directly. Medical staff here will keep ye under observation, and security will be very tight. When ye're ready, catch a shuttle down."

He handed me a datapad. "Travel expenses are credited on this. Ye'll find instructions also. Read 'em verra carefully and commit them to memory."

* * *

Not that I had very much to my name apart from the credits banked away in my account, which I could access from any GalCop station. There isn't that much room in a Sidewinder, and just carrying around my Macrae uniform had roughly doubled my personal possessions; but of course all that was gone along with my usual off-duty clothes and the very small handful of odds and ends I'd bothered taking around with me. I didn't shed too many tears over any of that, but it did mean I had nothing to stand up in apart from hospital pyjamas, which cover the essentials decently enough but look odd in public –

And I say that in spite of the wild variety of styles and colours you'll see on any GalCop station, where you'll find an awful lot of sentient species rubbing shoulders with each other, and even the humans are dressed according to a thousand different styles from a thousand different worlds. You'd think against all that background noise that hospital scrubs would go unnoticed, but they're almost uniform enough to be recognised for what they are anywhere you go, and unless you want to look like an escaped patient, you need to get something more fit to wear once you start thinking of checking out.

I had an escort wherever I went – actually a choice of escorts, who took turns to stick to me real close. The first one I was conscious enough to recognise told me to call him Nobby, since he figured that having pulled me from the æthereal void he was entitled to consider me family or near enough. Obviously I'd ask him why he was called Nobby, and he laughed and explained as follows:

"When we were kids together, we always had it drummed into us. *Noblesse oblige.* Means a chap has duties to go with the rank, what? Well, I always pronounced it with a short 'o', so those clever coves started calling me 'Nob-less', which I, you know, strenuously dissuaded 'em from until at least we compromised on 'Nobby'. Of course a Marquess is about as nobby as it gets from the perspective of *oi polloi*, but no more than an Earl in real terms. Anyway, you might as well call me it if you're going to be kicking around with The Macrae."

He also said he was happy to answer to Freddie or Pole, as the spirit moved me – and that, along with his effortless ability to pronounce the æ in "æthereal", won me over pretty much on the spot.

Pole was younger than Macrae, but still quite a bit older than me – old enough to have been my father if he'd had an early education, which from what I've learned about the Ususor nobility is as like as not – and from his colour and the strength of his grip and how he moved I guessed he didn't sit around all day doing nothing, whatever a Marquess might do for a living. I noticed a couple of things; firstly, that he was keeping me on the Ususor side of the Coriolis station rather than the GalCop side, and secondly, that without being ostentatious about it, he seemed to be armed to the teeth.

I learned very soon that this is a privilege which the ruling classes on Ususor negotiated with GalCop, along with a larger-than-usual share of the Coriolis station territory. The planet itself may be low-tech, and you might think it would be backward, but the nobility have a lot more influence within and around GalCop than you'd expect for all that, not least because they mainly have a lot of wealth tied up in the more advanced systems in their local cluster.

What it meant to me, at that time, was that it was perfectly safe for me to go shopping on the Ususor side, because if anyone had got past the rest of the station security, Freddie and the gang (as he also called them) had a number of interesting and effective ways of registering their objections to any threat on me.

Although my savings were a long way from allowing me to retire, they were more than up to buying a new wardrobe without the least danger I'd miss the money, and the only reason the tailor couldn't provide me with a whole new Macrae rig off the shelf was that they were most insistent about making it afresh from scratch. That, so they said, was the way the Macrae would want it, and the delay would be only a short one.

That did give me time to meet the other three – Swotty Neville, who was about as bookish as an Inleusian spotted wolf, Ginger Percy, who was exactly as red-haired as advertised, and

Stiffy Fitzalan –

"You see, back when I was learning to fence, the duelling-master was always on at me to loosen up. 'Too stiff! Too stiff!' he used to yell at me... so of course these dear souls made sure I heard plenty about it. As long as you know. These jesters would as soon have you believe it's because I never saw eleven a.m. without a stiff one to brace me up."

As I was to learn, all four of my rescuers could put away as much as Macrae and show as little sign of it – which would have put any spacer-bar partygoer to shame – but none of them were anything but cold sober the whole time they were watching me. But I was soon fit and well, and respectably dressed, enough to catch the shuttle down to the planet.

"Mind you don't forget what The Macrae told you to say, now," they warned me. "Hope to see you soon!"

All four of them claimed they needed to be there to see me board the shuttle. If there'd been anyone present who meant me harm, there wouldn't have been enough left to cremate. I hoped I'd see them again.

* * *

Ususor spaceport doesn't have a shanty town.

Now, I'm not claiming that Ususor or any other planet that's run by a noble class is automatically a paradise on the strength of it, and maybe a whole lot of people are worse off for not being allowed to leave their land when they want to. What I do know is that on my homeworld, people could leave their land because no-one cared enough to stop them, and they could travel all the way to the one advanced, civilized place on the whole planet, and then they could find out the truth when they got there. The streets aren't paved with gold, food and luxuries don't drop down from the sky by magic, and it's nearly impossible to find even a paying job that will keep you out of the most horrible squalor imaginable, and anyone there that can make a living off someone even worse off than them will cheerfully do so. So the fact that Ususor is spared that is automatically one up to the ruling classes.

There is a town not too far from the spaceport, and it does provide labour for them, and it does have an actual stone keep overlooking it, and there is a knight or a lord or someone in charge of the keep and the town, and it's his say-so as to whether anyone gets to move in to town, and strays and vagabonds are sent home either with a whipping or without one, as they choose – so Macrae told me later. But the town is no more disgraceful than anywhere else on the planet, and the human misery there is a drop in the bucket next to the shanty town on my homeworld.

Macrae's instructions told me to look for the sign of the thistle – with an illustration helpfully provided on my datapad, or I'd not have known what to look for – rendered in white on a midnight blue background. That took a little finding. There turned out to be a lot of signs of one kind or another, which shouldn't surprise anyone to learn since any given nobleman on Ususor rules only a small fraction of the planet. Still, once I'd learned what the sign looked like for in its actual size and colour, I had no real problems following it.

I was respectably dressed in my new Macrae colours, only a few hours old, and carrying one small holdall which contained all my other worldly goods. It came as no surprise to find that the young man on the desk under the sign of the thistle was dressed about the same – although the colours were different, the style and pattern were much what Macrae himself wore. Well, I had my instructions to follow.

"May I ask the purpose of your visit, please?" said the young man with perfect grace and politeness, and I answered:

"I'm here to see The Macrae."

"The Macrae?" he echoed.

"Yes. Macrae Of That Ilk, if you prefer," I replied. The message had deleted itself from my datapad after I'd read it, but Macrae had been quite insistent: All would be well if I used that form of words; and if I did not, then I would be given the politest run-around possible until I gave up and went away. I needed to get it right first time and I would not be given the slightest chance of a do-over. Fortunately, I'd remembered my lines correctly.

"Just so," said the young man. "May I ask if you are familiar with a low-technology planet?"

I smiled. "I was born and bred on Qudira. It doesn't get any lower than that, believe me."

He checked the computer screen in front of him and nodded. "So I see. Then you will need to know that GalCop credits cannot be redeemed in the interior, and you will need local currency. I have that here for you, if I may check... Thank you."

It was quite a novel experience to be handed a bag of actual coinage. My datapad beeped as the credit was transferred, and also as a guide was uploaded to tell me what the various coins were and how much they would buy. Then: "If you'll go with this young lady, please. Your transport's paid for."

The young lady in question led me through to a ground vehicle not unlike the one I'd ridden with Agent Elus in, but with seating for many more people. Today, though, I had it all to myself. If it came to that, there weren't too many single travellers coming through the terminal building, though it looked like it could accommodate many more if it had to.

There were several different air vehicles all marked with the thistle, too, some of them much larger than the one I was led to, though I can't tell you much more about them. I'm a spacer; all atmosphere transport is "thing with wings" as far as I'm concerned, and all I needed was to be shown where to get in and where to sit. This one had seating for just three other than the pilot. Apart from that, I can't tell you much, except that it definitely wasn't of local manufacture: its power plant was a slightly smaller version of what they put in an Adder, and there's no way Ususor's own industry was able to build that.

There wasn't much formality about our departure, either – much less than you'd need to launch from or dock with a Coriolis station even on a slow day. So I guessed they didn't have all that much use for air transport on Ususor, either.

However it was, I sat back and enjoyed the ride. The drive was a little less noisy than it would be in a Sidewinder, and there was a little noise as we were moving in air and not space. Otherwise, there was no reason not to just enjoy the view – except that the weather wasn't cooperating.

* * *

It rains a lot in the Highlands.

That was nothing I wasn't used to from Qudira, which has heavy rainfall for a lot of the year. On the other hand, on Qudira I'd never had to worry much about not being able to see more than ten metres in front of my face. I never travelled far enough from home to have to worry about getting lost or falling over the edge of a cliff, and at walking speed even ten metres of visibility is plenty to avoid bumping into things.

Air travel is different. I didn't enjoy the sensation of being unable to see anything in front of me for a good five minutes after we took off, and while we were then above the cloud layer and could see in front of us, I hadn't a clue what was below us.

My pilot seemed happy and confident though, and after half an hour or so she took us back down through the cloud, until we emerged a lot closer to the ground than I liked. To either side of us, in fact, the ground was reaching all the way up to the low cloud, which left me wondering uneasily what would have happened if she had been half a kilometre off to either side.

"Forecast has this clearing by the afternoon," she said companionably, "and then you'll get a better look. On landing approach now."

And with that she sleighted us directly at a long narrow lake below, which made me actually yelp in protest given that I was already looking around for a flat stretch of land and not seeing one. She took her eyes off the landscape long enough to look tolerantly at me. "Something the matter?"

"We're heading for the water!"

"Aye, so I should hope. Sit tight." And with that she went back to her task, performing a number of technical things that I would have understood better on a spaceship.

We touched the water about two minutes later, bounced once, then settled comfortably, leaving a white wake behind us. Look, I already told you they were just things with wings to me, all right? I had no idea the funny-shaped things below us were meant to float.

My pilot brought us round to a wooden jetty that stuck a hundred metres out into the lake, where they winched out a kind of cover that meant I could get off the aircraft without getting rained on, and the two young men waiting in a shed at the jetty were both stood on guard. I told them, as I'd told the young man at the spaceport, that I was there to see The Macrae, and one of them said:

"Scots, wha hae wi' Wallace bled;"

"Scots, wham Bruce has often led," I answered.

"Welcome to your gory bed," said the other.

"Or to victory!" I completed. They looked at each other, and the second one said:

"Was that 'often' or 'aften' she said just then?"

"Sounded like 'often' to me," said the first; and they looked at each other as though they were about to tell the pilot to take this stranger back where she belonged, before grinning and saying together "It'll do."

"And ye'd better come in the dry while we sort you out," the first one added. "Ah'm Andy, by the way. Andy McCorquodale. The fright yonder is Gordon, Gordon Farquhar. He disnae bite; me either."

They found me a warm place to sit while we waited for the rain to ease off, which it did just before noon, when Andy walked me along the jetty to where a two-horse carriage was waiting. I knew what a horse looked like, of course, although we had used an ox for the draft work when I was younger. The driver was a rather older woman than my pilot, but I didn't think she could be much over thirty, and I noticed that Andy seemed to defer to her.

"Welcome," she said kindly. "You'll be The Macrae's guest. Allow me to help you up; you've arrived just in time for the best of the day."

As he held the carriage door for me, Andy coughed discreetly. "It's the custom to spare your porter a mite o' siller – mebbe a groat or a bawbee."

I searched his honest face for any sign this was another joke at the stranger's expense, but I had money to spare and handed over two of the small silver pieces, reasoning that Gordon might expect a share, before the carriage pulled away.

The road would have passed for a fair highway on Qudira, but probably nowhere else, and the horses took it at a steady walk while the sky continued to clear. Now at last I could take in the grand sweep of the tree-lined hills flanking the long lake on either side – a deep green that was almost blue, with a hint of mist as the morning rain began to burn off again. And the scent! After the sulphurous atmosphere of my homeworld – which as a native you learn to endure but never love – and the carefully neutral air of every GalCop space station, this was almost beyond describing. I can only say that if it was possible to bottle "fresh", that would the the Ususorian Highlands scent – as if the world had been newly made that morning.

But the massive stone building in front of us, half an hour from the jetty, was not newly made by any means; and even the strange music being played by the four dozen kilted men marching on the gravel before it sounded ancient – inspiring awe and reverence in the same measure as it seemed to make the blood burn for battle. And there on the steps of the great stone house was Macrae, in full dress, but this time with an actual sword belted at his waist.

"Welcome," he said as the carriage driver helped me alight. "I hope you like the pipes!"

* * *

There was one thing puzzling me.

Which is a gross distortion of the truth. There were any number of things puzzling me, and I figured I might now have permission to ask, which Macrae confirmed at once.

"Aye," he said. "You're here no longer as my employee, but as a guest and a friend, so ask away."

He led me up the steps to the huge wooden doors, which a servant opened as we approached, and I got my first look inside. The overwhelming impression was of age – and space; it was far larger than any house I'd ever seen even if it was much smaller than many an office building you can see in a spaceport or most hi-tech planets. Inside, a fantastic assortment of art treasures and antiques lined the entrance hall, and old-fashioned pictures – the kind that were worked by a human being, not a computer – gazed down on us from either side. There was a queue of people waiting for us, or for Macrae at any rate.

"Thank you. You told me you were from Gerete?"

"And here I am settled into a large estate on Ususor, a couple of light-years away. Yes?"

I nodded. "That's exactly it. Also, why do people keep talking about 'The Macrae'? It's not just your sporting friends."

Macrae led me past the line of people. "Donald Hamilton, my majordomo. Ye've met his wife Elspeth already – she drove you up from the loch. Finlay Macadam, my ghillie. Sholto, Dirk, Morna and Shona, house-servants. That was Dougal that opened the door for us. And here comes the Young Macrae with Eilidh Campbell."

The Young Macrae was a copy of his father about thirty years younger, leaner and fitter but plainly cut from the same cloth. The girl with him was maybe a year or two younger than him, and the skirt she wore was of the same design as mine and the women of the Macrae household but a completely different colour pattern. She looked at me guardedly as we moved away.

"So to your questions," Macrae said. "Gerete is where I

live and spend most of my time when I'm not in space; it's where my company headquarters and what you might call my 'town house' are, and if you were looking to get hold of me for any reason, Gerete is where you'd start looking and where I'd be likeliest to see you. However: Here on Ususor is what you might call the 'ceremonial home' of all the Scots on Gerete. There are a few million that live here permanently, and many more that make the trip over from Gerete perhaps once or twice in their lives. It's actually a similar story with Percy, Fitzalan and the rest of them, though they're not Scots."

"Okay, and Scots are…?"

Macrae laughed. "The easiest thing for you to do is watch and listen. It's a way of dress, a way of talking, a way of life… it's blood-ties going right back to the Homeworld and it was old then. You'll see plenty of what it means over the next few days – while The Macrae is at home."

He waved me to a seat by a small table and called over two of the house-servants, Shona and Morna, both of them rather older women. "Miss Marilee just arrived from off-world. She will be wanting refreshment."

"All right," I said when they had left, "and The Macrae is, what, head of the family?"

"Of the clan – which is a collection of closely-related families. The men you met a few moments ago are not members of the Macrae family, but they are members of the clan – so Finlay might introduce himself as 'Finlay Macadam of Macrae', whereas I am 'Alisdair Macrae of Macrae', family and clan. Ye might call me 'Macrae Of That Ilk', meaning 'of the same' – another way of saying 'Macrae of Macrae', in other words." He frowned. "Although there's some scholarly controversy as to whether we're usin' the word in the exact ilk sense as our forefathers."

I sat back and listened to the music outside, letting the Scots atmosphere wash over me. It was yet another wonder Macrae had shown me in the few short days since I had met him. "This is fantastic."

"So we think also – and folks on Gerete will save all their lives to make the trip. Space travel's no' so cheap, even for a beggarly couple of light-years. But have no fear. Any that wants can register for a free trip, though the waiting list is very long and not everyone can arrange to come while The Macrae is at home."

Refreshments arrived – a hot herbal drink that was tan-coloured and had a hint of bitterness, and a plate of some cream-coloured biscuits that melted as you bit them. "What is happening, then? I'm guessing it's a very special occasion if the head of the clan himself doesn't come here very often."

"An astute deduction. There will be music, dancing, feasting, an opportunity for the townsfolk to see some traditional crafts and perhaps take home a little something as a keepsake, and the games of course. And also..." He leaned forward and rested his hand on one knee. "A few extra guests to discuss what I hinted at the other day, concerning that new ship I showed you. You're invited."

Macrae sat back in his chair. "Meanwhile, I have some father and son time owed to me with the Young Macrae, which means you will need showing around. Since that means taking young Lachlan away from his Campbell girl for an hour or two, I think perhaps you and she should make friends. I do believe..."

He cupped his hand to his ear and nodded. "Aye, they'll be in the music room just now. I hear the piano; that's Eilidh's playing for sure. Just cut along and let Lachlan know I want to see him, will you? You can follow the sound easily enough, I'm thinking."

* * *

Strange customs can sometimes be troublesome.

I didn't know what a piano was, but I heard the music coming from inside the house and guessed I could follow it through easily enough, and I found Lachlan standing by a black wooden box that I could have climbed into, and Eilidh sat in front of it working its control panel or whatever you call it. It was a long white board that ran the width of the box, divided into sections a bit thicker than my thumb and with black studs above it in irregular groups. How Eilidh knew what to do with them was more than I could say, since they weren't labelled or anything, but the sounds the box was making were recognisably musical even though they weren't like any music I knew.

"Good afternoon," I said, with an apologetic look for interrupting. "I wasn't told if I should call you Lachlan or Young Macrae, but your father would like to see you, please."

He bowed, a little stiffly, which made me wonder if I'd got the forms wrong, but I guess a summons from The Macrae counted higher than staying and correcting me, and he left me with Eilidh Campbell. She carried on playing for a few moments before turning and favouring me with a look, though by no means a friendly one.

"Do you shoot?" she asked.

"For a living, since you ask – although I'm not sure you mean with a ship's laser. I've tried out a gun or two and did all right with them."

Her perfect eyebrow tilted slightly. "Just so. You're from space, then?"

"Yes," I answered, guessing that it might be as well not to argue over the wording. "Does it show?"

"You're plainly no Macrae or even a Scot, I can see that much," Eilidh said. "How about fencing? Have you ever used a sword?"

I shook my head for no, and she said, "Very well, space girl. Then let me warn you that if I catch you making eyes at Young Macrae, I shall be in duty bound to call you out, and as it's a love matter I should be entitled to call for the weapons of my choice – and I'd be obliged to pink you at the very least."

It seemed wisest to bite my lip on the flip retort that sprang to mind, and instead I said, "Thank you for the warning, but I only just arrived, I've never seen Lachlan - "

Her hiss would have done Maussa proud, and I hastily

amended, "due apologies, never seen the Young Macrae before in my life and I've no ambitions there, I can promise you that."

She seemed to weigh up my reply for a moment or several, before giving me a nod and holding her hand out. "So that's understood, then, and I think we will do very well together. You said you shoot?"

"I have used guns – shot and bullet both, during my training," I said.

"There's a shoot planned for tomorrow. You should come," Eilidh said.

I supposed that meant we were friends after all, and after playing me another tune or two on the piano, Eilidh undertook to walk me round the grounds a bit. There were huge tents going up all around the grounds, and someone busily marking out what seemed to be a sports arena – the first I'd seen other than on a viewscreen in a bar – as well as livestock being driven into pens and some of them being slaughtered. I was used to the sight of a meat animal being put to the axe, but it came as a slight surprise to see that Eilidh took it in her stride as well.

Whatever a Macrae clan gathering might look like, it was plain there were going to be a lot of people present. Macrae hadn't mentioned how many clans there were or how many visitors to expect from Gerete, but the preparations looked like they were expecting thousands, maybe tens of thousands.

After a long tour of the grounds, Eilidh escorted me back to the house, and I found myself inspecting the art treasures in the entrance hall once again. There was a display of ancient weapons, including several swords similar to the one Macrae was now wearing, but also a great many unusual objects from all over the galactic cluster. Nothing from Qudira, naturally; our culture didn't inspire us to make many beautiful things, much less anything an outworlder would pay good money for.

The pictures entranced me. I looked closely at them to see what they were made of and ended up no wiser, but they showed – I supposed – many generations of Macraes in their finery, and whoever had worked the pictures had very cleverly captured something vital about each of them.

One in particular caught my eye. She was, maybe, somewhere between my age and Eilidh's; I didn't think she could be very much older. But she had an air of grace and authority about her that didn't seem to belong on such a young woman, and I seemed to notice that rather than simply the fact that she was a very beautiful woman. For whatever reason, her picture was set aside from the others, in a little alcove with a pair of tall candles for light.

I would have liked to ask Eilidh about her, but she'd gone her way, and I looked around to see if there was anyone to ask. As it happened Donald Hamilton was just passing through, and he very kindly interrupted his business to help me.

"I see you've noticed our Lady," he said.

"She's like a queen," I breathed. "Will she be at the gathering?"

Hamilton shook his head gravely. "Only in spirit. Just six months after this was painted, she visited The Macrae on Gerete. Her transport was attacked on her return to this system, and there were no survivors. Which explains adequately why The Macrae hates space pirates so."

* * *

When Eilidh said there was a shoot planned, she meant that she was in charge of it.

That, I guess, showed me how high she stood in Macrae society given that she was a Campbell girl herself – which is underselling her, since I found out she was The Campbell's eldest daughter. The Scots pass over any daughters in favour of sons when it comes to inheriting property and titles, but that doesn't make the girls any kind of meek milk-and-water little misses, by any means, and from the manner in which she was politely but firmly ordering the Macrae staff around, it was plain she had had plenty of practice.

She had some complimentary things to say about how I handled a shotgun before we were done, with a large bag to be sent down to the house for the enjoyment of the many guests, and she was no slouch herself in that department either. If Young Macrae and she were serious – as seemed to be the case – he was getting himself an all-action girl as far as I could see.

By the time we were returning and the beaters were being paid off and given their pick of the game to take home, there were already a great many people arriving. I'd noticed a number of aircraft descending on the "loch" (as Macrae called it) during the course of the day, and they were much bigger than the one I'd arrived on. Some more seemed to have been touching down further away, too, still within a long day's walk, and each group, I noticed, led by a piper.

"Aye," Macrae confirmed when I caught up with him later, "that's part of the deal for the off-worlders. Many of 'em haven't seen a real piper in their lives, and being landed in the Highlands and having one of their own to march 'em down to the gathering is the real start of the holiday for 'em. Most o' the flying boats aren't mine, by the way; we charter from each other, the various families, when it's festival time, aye, and from the southerners too. It all works out fair in the end."

When the gathering took off in earnest, with so many thousands of people assembled I couldn't properly guess at it, and the pipers by now mustering well over a hundred, Macrae took the platform, for he had an announcement for the crowd.

"Here before you all," he called out, "duly representative of Clan Macrae, it is my duty and my joy to announce to you the betrothal of Young Macrae and The Campbell's Daughter, and may their union be long and filled with happiness."

When the cheering died down, Macrae continued, "In recognition of my son's manhood, I declare to you that he and his betrothed are now the Lord and Lady of this gathering, and I step aside to bid him take his place!"

More cheers, and the young couple dressed in their

finery took centre stage and were ceremonially seated together; but while I was watching the festivities, Macrae slipped up to me and said, "Join me in the carriage. We've business of our own with a few friends."

I was surprised to find that the carriage already contained a transparent tank big enough to hold a man, though what it actually held was by far the biggest lobster I had ever seen, a deep indigo hued monster with bulging eyes that peered at me with disconcerting awareness. "Meet Hugh Fitzroy-Badgerson – not his real name, of course. Hugh's name isn't pronounceable, and I don't just mean by humans. He talks by changing his colour, and the name's one he picked out of a list. Hugh Fitzroy-Badgerson, let me introduce Marilee."

The commset in the lobster's tank shimmered barely noticeably, and the lobster himself changed colour momentarily in response. "Marilee is nearly as ugly as you. Which pronoun is appropriate?"

"No manners," Macrae commented. "Which is a mere statement of fact. Hugh's a Bierlese indigene, and they have trouble even understanding why humans would not want to say the first thing on their mind. Take comfort it's not meant for insult. Hugh Fitzroy-Badgerson, Marilee is a female of my species."

"Understood. Are you breeding with her?"

Macrae snorted and said "Let's think ourselves fortunate that the translator said 'breeding with'. Hugh Fitzroy-Badgerson, I am not. Marilee is present because she is a spaceship pilot who shoots pirates."

"Good," said the lobster. "Pirates should be shot. All pirates should be shot."

The floatplane waiting for us looked like the one I'd arrived in, but if the same pilot had flown it in, she had gone off-duty. Andy and Gordon were still there, though, and set to work to hoist Hugh's tank aboard, while the lobster's translator was unemotionally telling them what a pair of bumbling incompetents they were. Macrae didn't so much as crack a smile, but when they were done he handed each of them a purse of silver.

"There'll be no more traffic through today in either direction," he said. "Ye'd better be enjoying the gathering."

Macrae fiddled with the controls for a minute or two before take-off – balancing the weight of Hugh's tank by flooding the forward compartments of the floats, he said, although I got lost as to why this was necessary – and soon we were skimming low above the ground.

"We've not far to go," he said, "at least by air. Too bad ye're missing the gathering, but duty before pleasure – and ye'll enjoy what I have planned instead or I miss my guess."

In less than a quarter of an hour I found myself looking down into a low wide valley between gently-sloping hills. There was a lake below with a flying boat moored near one bank, and at the last minute as we descended I suddenly noticed a double row of spacecraft lined up in a long field. They were the craft Macrae had shown me at Diedar – twenty of them!

* * *

I couldn't think why I hadn't spotted the ships on the approach.

Macrae answered that question without prompting. "Reactive camouflage. Sensors in the belly pick up the colour and texture of the ground below, and the hull texture changes to mimic it. Power drain is minimal. Out in space ye'll mainly fade to black, but if you're in close to an asteroid your albedo will change to match the rock's. Might well buy you precious time especially if you're close enough in to the asteroid that your mass trace overlaps it."

"Nice," I said. "What're these ships called? I don't remember you telling me."

"Claymore," he said. "Which is Scots for 'dirty great sword', though again, as with 'of that ilk', the greybeards are still arguing as to the correct and authentic usage from antiquity. But whichever way you slice it, it's a darned fine name for a ship and I'm faintly surprised no-one's ever used it before."

While he was explaining this, Macrae taxied the aircraft to the shore where it sat, rocking gently on the water, while someone rowed out from the bank and made it fast to a mooring. There was a bigger boat already on the way out with a small crane on the foredeck, which they used to transfer Hugh's tank across while Macrae leapt nimbly onto the after deck and held his hand out to me.

On the shore, near the moorings, was a rather smaller house than Macrae's mansion, but still far bigger than what I'd grown up in. Smoke was curling up from its chimneys and I could see a number of people going in and out. They were all in Macrae clothing – but then, so was I, and I could see one or two who plainly weren't locals, such as the giant whose skin was a livid crimson and whose head bore a pair of short horns that looked as though they belonged on a bull. I scanned him discreetly with my datapad, which identified him as a native of Gelegeus.

I was itching for a closer look at the Claymores, but it would have to wait for now. Hugh's tank was transferred to a push-cart that four strong men could manage, and punctuated by the lobster's constant stream of complaints we all made our way for the house. Inside, there was a large hall laid out for a lecture rather like the ones I'd known as a trainee, with some higher-tech facilities than Ususor could boast of generally. I guessed Macrae must have imported them from Gerete, which was well up to making display screens and the like.

There was a raised dais at the front of the hall, with a lectern to one side. Hugh Fitzroy-Badgerson, still complaining at the treatment, was transferred to the dais, while Macrae took his place at the lectern. I looked around for a seat in the hall, and found myself near the Gelegeusian with a more human-looking girl to the other side.

"Are we all here yet?" came Macrae's amplified voice. Someone else was patched into the system too, as a different voice came over the same speaker.

"One more transport inbound from the spaceport, sir. On finals now."

"All right. Have out the refreshments while we're waiting. Make a note of where you're sitting, ladies and gentlemen, and be ready to go in fifteen minutes."

That left me barely time to grab a hot drink and another of those Scots biscuits I was fast developing a taste for, and to trade a quick hello with some of my fellows. There was no-one else there that I knew, but I saw a pattern forming with the few I had time to speak to: they were all escort pilots like me. I wondered what exactly Macrae had in mind.

When the last arrivals came in I spared them a quick glance – a young man and a slightly older one, both in Macrae costume, and I looked away again. Then I blinked and looked back.

Terek!

But whatever might have brought him here, I wasn't to find out for now. Macrae had the lights dimmed and everyone seated, then turned towards the tank and said, "We're all ready now. Hugh Fitzroy-Badgerson, will you begin?" And everyone sat spellbound and listened to a talking lobster.

"You have today's agenda on your datapads," he announced. "To begin with I shall discuss the effects of the pirate problem on the galactic economy, together with historically recent trends.

"You should understand that I have been retained by Macrae because of my expertise in a number of fields, including economics and game theory. Additionally, I shall apprise you later of some recent technical developments that will be of great value in the course of action we are proposing today. But first, the economy."

It was not encouraging to listen to, and Hugh had a great many fact-sheets and graphs to get his point across. The plain fact, as he argued it, was that the galactic economy was a frail creature, and had been for many years, but had suffered a recent downturn. It was now – or so the lobster's facts and figures seemed to show – nearing the critical point at which piracy was becoming able to grow faster than the economy could support measures to suppress it.

"Or to go to medicine for our metaphor, the infection itself is breaking down the patient's immune system, which – in my species as well as in yours – is a recipe for a dead patient. True, the disease organism itself will then die; but that will be small comfort to the patient, and the disease itself is deaf to reason."

As though anything needed to make matters worse, Hugh pointed out what would happen when the economy finally went belly-up. The Navy was already under-funded and over-stretched. Once the Galactic Cooperative couldn't sustain itself or the Navy any longer, we wouldn't even get the chance to bootstrap ourselves again. Thargoids would see to that.

* * *

Macrae had something of his own to say.

After Hugh's encouraging state-of-the-galaxy address, our host took over with a presentation of his own: "Hired Escorts – A Service in Crisis". He said that what was mostly concerning him was morale:

"And by that you're not to understand that I've got one bad word to say about the courage of the young men and women who are dedicating their lives to seeing that commerce is allowed to take place. Far from it. I've seen that at first hand and I have plenty of reliable witnesses to back me up. You and your peers are giving of your all and your bravery is top-quality, believe me.

"But what concerned me to begin with – what concerns me the more I look into it – is that your hope appears to be fading over time. Part of that is no doubt a realistic assessment of your survival chances since the pirates started getting smarter and various organised crime factions started demanding a bigger piece of the pudding. But it's not just that. You have precious little, what they call *esprit de corps*, left to you any more. That's eroded, and it's been replaced by a kind of hopeless bravado mixed with hedonism and whatever swagger it takes for you to get through another day waiting to die.

"I don't say that I blame you. Many of us have hit rock bottom where hope's concerned, and we've had to cling to whatever we could find to try to get us through it, and some of us have made it, and some of us have not. But that's not the spirit that has lent itself to staying alive, fighting another day successfully and remaining intact as an operational unit; and history's on my side on this, a thousand times over."

He showed us some examples from old records, some going back supposedly to the Homeworld itself, and they certainly seemed to bear him out. What he charitably described as a Service-with-a-capital-S was becoming another legion of the damned, and while history records these as dying gloriously and giving the other side a hard time in the process, it didn't make up for the fact that they did end up dead and losing a lot of experience and expertise when they went.

"Part of the problem, of course, is that while I call you a Service, you cease to be one the day you quit training. After that, you have a fighting ship to which you've been sponsored, and you're left to your own devices. No further logistics, strategy, tactics; no command structure, no unit identity, not even a uniform. You fund yourselves out of the piecework you do, and you sink or swim as you're able." Macrae shook his head. "I'll not speak ill of those who founded this scheme, but in practical terms it's not working out. Take a break, ladies and gentlemen, and then Hugh Fitzroy-Badgerson will have some more insights to share."

I managed to meet Terek while we were helping ourselves to lunch. He smiled at me a little nervously and a little apologetically, which was only to be expected but unnecessary.

"It's all right," I said. "I found someone to talk it out with, and now I understand. I didn't like it much at the time, but

I know you were doing it for the best, and you may well have been right."

He grimaced. "Maybe. But I was feeling pretty near rock bottom a few days later. Stumbled into someone at Qube who said he had a long run coming up and would appreciate a travelling companion and someone to drink with off duty – and he used to be an escort back before he made enough to upgrade and get out, so he still had his pass to the bar. We got talking, and he said he had somewhere to visit that I might enjoy if I didn't mind dressing different to fit in with how they do things here. Looks like the same happened to you."

I smiled. "Looks like it did. And… the day's not been cheering so far, but I've a kind of a hunch they're going somewhere with this."

And of course they were. Hugh's next offering was "The Tactical Deficiencies of the Escort System", on which he was blunt and to the point.

"History records, and theory further predicts, that an ambush seldom if ever results in a devastating rout for the ambusher. There are, of course, occasions when it turns out that he who believed he was the ambusher turns out to have been misinformed; but that's a failure of intelligence and planning, not a deficiency in the ambush stratagem.

"What you have now, almost invariably, is a trader and a string of guards in one of a number of predictable formations. Some work better than others but none is foolproof. That means that your attacker is invited to look you over, decide on their plan of attack, and execute it if the numbers and position are on their side. Sometimes they take some losses. More often you take worse losses. As long as the decision to engage and to disengage is in their hands, triumphs for your side will be rare."

Maps, records of old battles, facts and figures followed in almost bewildering succession. "At present, even if you win the occasional fight, the enemy simply retire until they are ready to re-engage with greater numbers and in more favourable circumstances."

"But what else can we do?" demanded someone – it was the Gelegeusian horned redskin. "We can't leave our freighters, and we're not a Navy strike team."

"Not yet," broke in Macrae – and I felt a thrill at those two words. "The Navy has its hands full anyway. But we have new ships, a promise of more, talented fighters in search of a soul… and, in short, all we need to take the offensive."

Disciplined until then, the meeting burst into a buzz of discussion.

* * *

Macrae gave the hubbub its head for a couple of minutes.

"Yes," he said, when order had been restored, "I'm quite serious about taking the offensive. Our aim is to begin taking the profitability and viability out of piracy in the most efficient manner possible, and I don't mean to waste good lives in doing it. Further, I have financial backing and many conditional pledges.

"Not even I am wealthy enough to have underwritten the entire squadron of Claymores awaiting you on the airstrip, but what I do have is the ear of a number of people who have wealth to spare and are sick and tired of seeing their prerogatives infringed upon. In short, if we can achieve sufficient success at the outset, we will see a great deal of money being released to further our endeavours. And concerning success, I'll hand over once more to Hugh Fitzroy-Badgerson."

"Quite right," said the lobster's commset. "It is from me that you now need to hear. You can achieve some success simply by conducting armed sweeps in force in systems known to suffer high levels of pirate activity. With twenty Claymores in skilled hands it would be nothing to dispose of a typical pirate formation efficiently and without loss or even serious danger. This, however, only scratches the surface of what you can do.

"It is orders of magnitude more efficient to destroy the

enemy's logistical capability and support framework. To date this has been difficult to achieve. Some pirates are able to disguise themselves as honest traders, and we can do little about this. Others however take the precaution of constructing base facilities where they can stockpile surplus cargo, undertake repairs, refuel and rearm – and launder their gains by shipping them out aboard craft with no known criminal record.

"Some pirate hideouts are in the remote corners of star systems, while others are on lawless planets themselves. To date these have been difficult to locate. That state of affairs need obtain no longer."

The screen displayed a piece of tech I didn't recognise in the slightest. "Artefacts recovered from pirate derelicts have been examined and reverse-engineered," Hugh Fitzroy-Badgerson continued. "This device might as well be termed a 'Pirate Compass'. If I need to explain further, you will not profit from the explanation."

"And while I'm not as tactless as our technical expert here – who has omitted to mention the identity of the genius who did the reverse-engineering – I'll just emphasise the main points again: We have a means of locating pirate concentrations. We have new ships capable of taking the fight to them in space or in atmosphere. We have wealthy backers who're not beholden to the whims of a government to see that, once our enterprise takes off, it can and will snowball," said Macrae. "Now, we have simulators configured for the Claymore specs and the first group can go try them out at once. The rest of you are welcome to take a look over the babies themselves, and I doubt me you'll be disappointed."

As we filed out, one of the attendants approached me and beckoned me aside. "Ye're offered the compliments of The Macrae, and his invitation tae dine a' his table the nicht. The Macrae seats hissel at seven-thirty punctually."

"Thank you," I said. "Please tell The Macrae I shall look forward to it."

I wasn't on the rota for the first turn in the simulators,

so I joined the fourteen others scurrying out, some more on their dignity than others but all eager to see the new ships. Most spacers will gladly look over a ship they haven't seen before, even if it's a rickety old Worm that can't mount a laser fit for more than a cat toy. But a new class of fighting ship, especially one with any kind of a novel feature such as atmospheric capability, will draw them like bees to an opening flower.

Although powered down, two of the Claymores were open for inspection so we could clamber over them, try the seat for size, and get the feel of how well laid out the cockpit was. There was even just enough room to slip out of the seat altogether, and rather more advanced plumbing than a Sidewinder boasted, so it looked like the hated space pants might be a thing of the past. I found the controls falling very naturally to hand and the interior looking almost like how you imagine a Fer-de-lance's flight deck. There was a definite air of build quality and polish that I wasn't used to.

For all that I looked forward to flying one of these, my mind was more than half on dinner with Macrae. It felt a little odd in prospect now that we were no longer shipowner and escort pilot – but I was confident Macrae would put me at my ease.

We got tired of looking over the ships after a while, and were itching for our turns at the simulators. I found myself on the last shift, and while it's not quite the same as flying a ship for real, it's a lot better than nothing. The Claymore felt fast and responsive, almost twitchy, but not uncontrollably so. Well, inherently unstable craft turn faster, so that was a plus point once you could learn to manage it. The sim included a spot of gunnery practice as well, which gave me notice that I was going to need the cross-training if I was going to hit anything reliably, but promised at the same time that once I trained my reflexes to the Claymore then I'd be able to get my sights on exceptionally quickly – and it came with some gunnery aids that the Sidewinder couldn't have matched.

I made sure it was well before seven-thirty by the time I

was dressed for dinner, wearing a small piece of gold jewellery on my blouse that had been left in my quarters. Macrae was dressed to the nines too, sword and all.

*   *   *

When I thought I had seen fine dining before, it turned out that I was mistaken.

Bearing in mind that this wasn't even the principal Macrae residence, I was stunned as much by the setting as I was by the menu. Neither the table nor anything on it could have been less than four or five hundred years old, and what wasn't solid silver or gold looked as though it was diamonds. If there were real kings anywhere in the galaxy or throughout history who'd taken their meals in more elegance than this, I was struggling to imagine it – even in the story books that we had very occasionally seen in the school when I was little.

Macrae, of course, wore it as to the manner born, as though everything he was sitting on or eating off was not a priceless antique; and as for the meal itself, well, I must have described Macrae's taste well enough by now. He said that the entire Eight has nothing to show more fair than the taste of wild Highland venison simply presented, although if that was simple presentation then it was a lifetime's skill to master. I was left groping vainly for superlatives. It was the kind of meal that makes you feel as though the rest of your life will be an anti-climax.

I was also introduced at last to the real, genuine Macrae whisky, and not just the second-best liquor Macrae was prepared to carry about with him as travel rations. It shone like liquid gold in the light of the candles and the sparkle of the cut crystal, and the scent... just inhaling it seemed to conjure the music of the pipes and the Macrae family gathering. "You've excelled even yourself, Commander Macrae," I said.

He laughed gently and easily. "No' so much of the Commander at the table, I think. I'm glad ye've enjoyed it. I've missed our little bit o' dinner together these last couple of days."

"To be honest I thought we'd be done with that now you were home again – and it's a delight to be mistaken."

"And also to have ye there. That wee bauble looks well on you, Marilee," he added, indicating the gold filigree clasp.

"It feels marvellous – like I'm wearing history. Is it very old?" I'd just managed to rephrase the question in time.

"Aye. It's no' been worn since my great-granny passed – and I was quite a stripling then." He sighed. "Well, the work's begun at last. It's been a time coming together. Are ye still in, or shall I write you up for a Cobra after all?"

I gave him a very direct look – more direct than I'd have dared before. "To be honest, I was still seriously considering the trading life until I heard you and your friend speak today. A free ship and the chance to make a fortune, maybe on the Isinor to Zaonce run, with injectors to run away from trouble… But what you're describing matters more than that."

"I promise you sincerely, I believe it in my heart. Whether we can or can't help civilization to hold off barbarism," Macrae said, "I'm convinced it's the fight we need to be fighting."

"And now I am too," I said. I looked out of the east window. "The moon's up. Can we see those lovely Claymores from anywhere in the house?"

"Aye. There's a drawing-room that overlooks the field." He rang for a servant to take my chair as I rose, just another piece of how the other half lived.

From either side of us, Macraes looked down over the centuries, and we stood together looking over the rows of gleaming Claymores, just visible in the moonlight and looking sleek and dangerous. Macrae sighed. "It will work. Hugh's a planning genius. This is going to make a difference."

"If it does," I said, barely above a whisper, "will you give yourself permission to rest?"

His head snapped around and I saw the set of his jaw

and the glint in his eye in the light of the fire in the drawing-room, and then he exhaled sharply through his nose and said "Ye know, then."

"I wasn't told that it was a secret. Sorry," I said; and then a streak of cussedness made me say, "Except not. Macrae, I've suffered too! I saw my whole family die, and some of them weren't dead when the fire started. So I know what it's like to try to work out the secret that will make the memory go away, believe me!"

My vehemence seemed to startle him. He was silent for a while and then said, "Aye. Ye've no' spoken out o' turn. And… aye, permission's a good word. I've wealth and power, as ye can see – an' I've spent twenty-four years trying to find how best to put them to work, an' in between times, makin' a few of the blighters pay." Except that he didn't say "blighters". "It's no' been enough yet. But… Take the larger view. This is a good undertaking for the sake of everyone, an' no' just tae help me sleep o' nights."

I turned to him. "You're a good man, Alasdair Macrae. And I'm yours for as long as this lasts."

I knew as soon as I'd said it that there was room to take that two different ways. I wasn't sure, straight away, whether Macrae had noticed it too. He turned and said, "You're a good one yourself, Marilee."

My hand was resting on the S-shaped back of a peculiar seat. "What's this?" I asked. Macrae grinned.

"It's called a 'love seat'. A young man and his maid can sit in it so they can face each other – ye see?"

"Perhaps it should be sat in," I said, taking one side for myself.

We looked at each other in silence for a few moments before what felt like irresistible magnetism pulled my face towards his, our mouths opening at the same instant.

* * *

At about midnight we both woke up enough to make our way from the hearthrug to the bedroom next door.

To be honest, just lying in front of a fire on a thick fur rug snuggled up to Macrae was a joy in itself, but the fire burned itself out after a while and it certainly wasn't summer in the Highlands. Besides, though moving felt like a bother at the time, it had its compensations: By the time we'd moved and got settled down comfortably we decided that we wanted each other again. If it wasn't as explosive as the first time, it was certainly warm, intimate and highly enjoyable, and it kept us both pleasantly worn out until the dawn started to creep through the curtains.

I was awake before Macrae was, and I lay there in silence for some time, just watching him and thinking. I'd been convinced I preferred girls – and I'd been quite happy not having much experience of boys to change my mind. It would be a tired old cliché to say that I'd just not met the right man before, but one thing was for certain, Macrae was pretty much the definition of a real man that they could cite in the encyclopaedia.

He came round with me watching him – and he came fully awake in a matter of seconds. My grin was mirrored by his, which didn't look so very much older than mine at that.

"Well," Macrae said, "that isnae how I was expecting last night to play out at all."

"Any regrets?" I asked. He laughed.

"Traditionally it's meant to be the man who asks the young lady that question. But no. Ye know, I dreamed of Eileen last night." Macrae grinned widely and in pure joy. "She said, 'Ye silly old fool, it's about time'. So I guess I did get around to givin' maself permission for somethin', after all.

"Aye well, another day, another load of things tae do. Best be movin', young Marilee."

"In a little while. But before you do, Macrae, you've one task that needs doing right away, here and now."

"Is there now?" He looked at me with the most impish

expression you could imagine. And then... he got on with the task at hand.

I'd guess that the house servants of a gentleman of rank are used to the idea, at least, of picking up tactfully after their lord and master when he's been entertaining a lady at short notice. However much or little Macrae might have required them to do so, they'd moved seamlessly into action by the time we found clean clothes and breakfast for two waiting for us. Macrae breakfasted lightly and much less elaborately than he dined, but we still found time to linger over one last hot drink and talk things over before the business of the day got under way.

I agreed with him that last night had caught me quite as much by surprise as it had him, and Macrae said, "Aye. But it feels right, Marilee. You and I, we couldn't have more different backgrounds, but – It's trite to talk of 'soul mates', but I've noticed, we seem to understand each other wi' hardly a word spoken."

"Yes. I've noticed that too. Last night, we seemed to manage to have a row and a reconciliation with not much more than a dozen words apiece. I said something, you reacted, I processed that and gave you my reaction in turn, and..."

"There we were, both of us feelin' we'd managed to say aye that needed to be said," Macrae finished, "which counts for a great deal. Slightly more, even, than a gorgeous young miss flingin' hersel' at me."

I pulled a face. "I'm an untutored farm girl from the arse-end of nowhere, and at best I might scrub up fit to be seen; but I've seen gorgeous while I've been a spacer, and I'm not it."

"Well, ye look well in Macrae tartan," Macrae said, "and I'm thinkin' that dinin' like a Macrae has done you naught but good. At any rate, to what extent gorgeous is in the eye o' the beholder, I'll say this much: there came a point last night when it would ha' taken a gun at my head tae keep me from kissin' ye."

"I think I could date that to the second," I said, "on the grounds that I was feeling the same way."

He grinned and quoted something about a tide in the affairs of men, which was a reference I didn't get, and then said, "At any rate – to business, and no more distracting me. We have some likely lads and lasses to train on Claymores today and for some time to come, and that includes you. Let's get to it."

Which leaves me fast-forwarding over the worthy but dull days spent in simulators starting to get used to the key features of the new ship, and to the much more interesting moment when I was sat in mine for the first time, with the drive up and running and the Claymore hovering a metre off the turf on its ground-effect thruster. The HUD had a number of displays that I wasn't used to, since I'd not flown an atmosphere-capable ship before.

Macrae's recorded voice was giving the tutorial. "Welcome aboard the Claymore, a new concept in space fighting that I am confident you will find enjoyable and a potent weapon all in one delightful package. In a moment your flight director is going to vector you onto a trajectory that will take you to the safe altitude of five thousand metres, where you can start to explore the capabilities of this lovely performer without either blundering into space traffic that you're not yet ready for or colliding with the ground, which is an experience you will not want to repeat. When you're ready, go."

* * *

At five thousand metres, the Claymore skimmed through the thin air above the cloud layer.

"You are now flying a ship that has been designed from the ground up to be fully capable in air or in space. The tactical edge this can confer on you in the right circumstances can hardly be described adequately in a few words, but you'll come to appreciate it as you gain experience. You've the beating of any pure airplane in performance at altitude, simply because he's designed to work with aerodynamic lift and you aren't. You can use it, but at height you can work like a pure space plane just when he's pinned between his stall speed and his Mach number. Don't worry too much about the theory for now, just remember: You can beat any airplane if you fly high and fast enough.

"Equally, any spaceship that follows you into air is going to be struggling. Re-entry heating is not a problem at your speed, but you're designed to be aerodynamically efficient and a ship like a Gecko or a Sidewinder is not. The thicker the air, the more the turbulent airflow is going to swamp his guidance systems, and once he departs, he's done for. So remember – on the borders of the sky, where it's not quite space and not quite air, you're the queen of the battlefield. And you'll be no slouch when you're clearly one side of the line or the other, either.

"Now let's go down into cloud and work on your orientation. You've an artificial horizon when you're in air. Pay attention to it and learn to love it as your dearest friend when you cannot see the ground. Manage your ship gently when you're in air, and she'll pay you back richly. Off you go now."

Our task was simple – maintain a straight course for fifty kilometres while remaining between three thousand and thirty-five hundred metres above ground. We were to disable the flight director but were free to use any other aids the atmosphere HUD offered us; and we found it difficult.

In space you have a clear unlimited view in all directions except straight into the sun, and you see any navigation hazards from at least twenty-odd kilometres away – a little less in the case of a cargo barrel or escape capsule, but the scanner flags those up for you anyway and it would be really hard to crash into one by mistake. And once you've pointed your ship where you want it to go, there's nothing to keep it from going there in a straight line.

Whereas in air your ship is always wanting to gain or lose height or wander off track to left or right, and a patch of cloud can cut your visibility to almost zero in moments. We still had the scanners to warn us of any solid objects in our airspace, including each other, and the HUD to at least provide us with the information we needed to keep us right way up and on the assigned bearing, but it took a few days before we could even complete the most basic of training exercises to Macrae's satisfaction.

It's also unnerving to be looking down at unbroken cloud from two and a half thousand metres, with orders to go down through the cloud until you're in clear air and the full knowledge that some peaks in the Highlands reach a good fourteen hundred, and your ship can cover the odd kilometre between those two limits in just a few seconds. Still, it taught us to take care, and once again, there turn out to be compensations. Even for a hardened spacer, there's a thrill in making a low fly-by that leaves a white trail in the loch below you, and then pulling up your nose at the end of the pass and making for the clouds like, as Macrae put it, "a homesick angel" with just a touch on the injectors taking you past twice the speed of sound in a vertical climb. You use injectors very gently in dense atmosphere, but you can use them.

I did comment to Macrae over dinner on the third evening that it was a shame to be missing the Macrae gathering, and he grinned.

"That's no lie – and I hope ye'll have the chance to see it another time, for it's worth the seeing and the hearing. But that's how it's got to be, and I'm sure you ken why."

"Of course," I said. "You need security for this exercise here, and so you've got the Macrae estates packed shoulder to shoulder with Scots from Ususor and Gerete both, and a stranger wouldn't pass for five minutes in a crowd like that; and meanwhile you've given yourself a perfect excuse to be somewhere else."

"Aye. My lad and the Campbell girl were ready to formalise their relationship anyway, so all we did was advance things a mite – and once that's been done, it is indeed traditional to let the Young Macrae take charge of an event like this, with no father peeking over his shoulder to be sure he's doing it right."

But my fellow trainees weren't allowed to suffer by

having to miss the gathering, for Macrae had laid on plenty of entertainment for them as well – pipers and dancers among them, and an instructor or two to teach them how to dance reels and flings and so on, and if I was the only one dining personally at the Macrae's table, the rest were getting fed and watered royally on their own account.

Macrae watched all of this with fond satisfaction. "These lads and lasses have been asked to do a hell of a job for a long while with no sense of belonging. Now – well, look at them."

I looked. It wasn't the wild desperate spacer partying I was used to. Something was changing.

* * *

Macrae was giving his handful of escort pilots a soul.

He was giving them a lot more besides, of course. The speed, firepower and flexibility of the Claymores was a large part of it – and also, and quite unlike the singleships we'd been used to, they oozed build quality and a level of comfort that made their pilots feel valued in a way that a Sidewinder never could. I'd felt a kind of rough affection for *Get An Honest Job*, sure enough, but I was growing to love *The Black Bear* for a hundred little added extras. A few extra grams of solid alloy billet here, a little rounding there, a few centimetres of cushioning on this and a few extra degrees of adjustment on that, even the recorded pipe music it played while the systems were being brought online... it all combined to make it feel like my ship.

Above all, the promise of a tactical objective that did not simply boil down to "Sit there in deep space until someone shoots at you, then you can start shooting back and we'll hope that being pure of heart will carry the day against an opponent who's been allowed to choose the battle and dictate the terms". Macrae had barely even shown me the notes on our planned operations, but he'd been happy to go over the broad aims with everyone: go out looking for pirates and for everything they needed to keep their vile business going, and descend on a point target with force overwhelming enough to wipe it out of existence.

"Of course," he murmured to me one night, as I lay with my head pillowed on his shoulder, "this isn't everything by a long shot. Ye can see for yourself that there's too much uniformity about pirate operations the Galaxy over for it to be small-time criminals on their own initiative. Depend on it, there are crimelords hidden away in respectable offices on high-tech worlds, running the whole show like a business and several tiers away from ever getting their own hands dirty. Well, but we can put a crimp in their balance sheet, at any rate."

But the Claymore Force was being grown and nurtured, adopted into the Macrae clan and taking on a group identity along with the tartan and the music and dancing – and they were taking it on eagerly, like a brood of adoptees looking for a mother and father. Well, the Macraes were up to providing that and no mistake.

"O' course, it was all done wi' blood ties back in the day. Someone's daughter would marry someone's son – aye, not unlike Young Macrae and the Campbell girl – and from then on, the new family was grafted on to the rootstock an' as much a part o' the clan as though it had always been there. Their fights became the clan's fights, and likewise the other way round."

"Is that what's happening with your son, then?" I said. "Are the Campbells now Macraes, or the Macraes now Campbells?"

"No, no," Macrae chiding, in the tones that told me I'd made a child's error although with a glint in his eye that assured me he was only teasing. "Campbells and Macraes alike are both weighty clans in their own right and they're staying that way. But this is how we strengthen the bonds of friendship at any rate – and bring in a little fresh blood into the noble families. It's understood that the Macraes have judiciously accepted that the Campbell girl is good enough for their son. On our side, that is. Of course, the Campbells put a different slant on it."

So over a course of some weeks, the Claymores became welded into a fighting unit, all of them dressing and carrying on as though they'd been Macraes all their lives, until one morning Macrae called us all to the flying field for what he called a "live exercise".

"There's a freighter due at the Witchpoint in two hours and thirty minutes from this time. She's unescorted and carrying cargo and passengers enough to draw all the hounds of Hell down on her head. You know what to do. Bring the *Quinquereme of Nineveh* in safely, bring yourselves back alive, an' don't let a single whipped cur get away if you have the choice."

I was second in line behind *Johnny Cope* as we powered up, with *Lochanside* next behind me and *Cock o' the North*, *Lovat's Lament* and *Mhairi's Wedding* following in succession. We hadn't chosen the names; they were Macrae's invention, or as he explained, drawn from ancient Highland tradition – and the names of the music each of our ships played on power-up. I could recognise my own in a few seconds when the pipers played it, and a few of the others well enough, though I couldn't yet tell all twenty apart; and, naturally, I was already ready and willing to explain to everyone why *The Black Bear* deserved pride of place.

We came out of atmosphere with the Claymores in triple column and the Coriolis station low down towards the sunlit horizon, in local afternoon and hard to see against the sun. At full normal speed it was a good hour out to the Witchpoint but we were in no hurry to waste injector fuel so full normal speed it was; Torus drive is no use to ships that are meant to stay in formation.

At the Witchpoint we cut power, some of us with an asteroid to loiter close by and others just hanging silent in space, in a wide ring normal to the plane of the ecliptic and face-on to the planet. Somewhere close by, but out of scanner range, other ships were up to something similar. We watched the minutes count down while we waited for *Quinquereme* to arrive in-system.

"He's here." The Bull's commset. "Stand by for

141

action."

It wasn't long in coming.

*   *   *

Macrae had not exaggerated when he'd spoken of "all the hounds of Hell".

Quinquereme of Nineveh was a Boa 2, although I hadn't a clue either what a quinquereme might be or where Nineveh was – it was no planet that I had ever heard of. Macrae was to put me straight on that later. But for now, as we IDed the ship and her captain, Commander Bill Voce, we had other things on our minds.

Passengers draw contract hits – the higher-profile the passenger and the more important his trip, the more attention the Assassins pay to him. Pirates are more interested in cargo. If the two turn up at about the same time, neither has the least objection to working with the other since their interests don't clash, and this can spell very bad news for the freighter captain.

Voce, by the look of things, had been in a scrap or two, and a Boa 2 can be outfitted with a lot of desirable goodies. We could immediately see one thing he hadn't skimped on. His drive flame flared brilliantly and he surged forward blisteringly fast for such a big ship, for a Boa 2 is far from stately and that goes double if she has injectors.

Quinquereme had blasted away even as the messages started coming over the commset: "There's Bill Voce now. Let's teach him that dealing with Eensti D'razzraq was a mistake!". But most of the assassins now converging on Voce had injectors too, so he'd done not much more than cut down the odds – and while a Boa 2 is a durable target with the proper upgrades, she's a large one too.

"Blue section, take the stragglers," said The Bull. We'd taken to calling him that because Gelegeusian is hard to pronounce and The Bull adapted to it easily once we'd mentioned the qualities that bulls are mainly associated with:

strength and courage. And we'd adapted easily to The Bull taking command of the Claymores once we'd reasoned that a leader who wanted the job was worth three who'd had to be persuaded to take it. Decisive instructions in good time are worth a lot; if they happen to be the right orders, then so much the better. Six Claymores headed for the injectorless assassins while The Bull himself pointed *The Rowan Tree* in the direction of the fleeing Boa 2 and her pursuers.

Claymores are fast. We were in time to see *Quinquereme*'s aft laser burn through an Asp's shields before he broke away, injectors still at full bore, which would normally have let him back off, cool his own shields and laser, and close in again while the freighter was still trying to swat the rest of his foes with a hot laser. But this time was different. *Johnny Cope* broke after him, locked on and opened up before the Asp had time to do more than scream "I'm taking heavy fire from the [Unknown_Ship]!" and burst into white fire.

"White section take them. Red section, watch for hostiles!"

We'd been warned to beware of pirates as well as assassins on this run and The Bull wanted some of us to have cool lasers when they arrived. But over in White section, we were more than willing to choose our own targets. We arrived in line astern, each of us settling quickly onto a target and letting it have the lot. The Claymore's laser was fully effective at twenty-five kilometres, but fifteen kilometres was the range I was used to and it was the range I opened up at, burning through a Cobra III without wasting a single megawatt. As usual the nuisance had a missile auto-locked and launched in the instant before he blew, and inevitably my first scream of ECM didn't put it down. I cut thrust to zero, auto-acquired the missile and confirmed it as a hardpoint. Too much of a risk to try to shoot it.

"*The Black Bear* here. Missile incoming. Breaking."

"Acknowledged. Lose it and get back when safe," said The Bull.

Losing it wasn't going to be a problem as long as I had

injector fuel to spare. But there was another collection of traces appearing and -

"Hello, Bill Voce. Today's toll is 10TC."

"In a pig's eye," sent *Quinquereme of Nineveh* – and he was slowing to bring his front laser to bear on the new arrivals. I was starting to like Commander Voce, all the more when his laser speared through the darkness straight into the Python who'd demanded the toll.

"Red section going in," sent *Bonnie Dundee*, Terek's ship. They were all fresh and hadn't wasted or taken so much as a shot yet. I was still watching the hardhead behind me, now spiralling on its final run before a touch on my injectors took me out of reach... and out of reach again... and again until it blew with what might have been frustration.

By now my laser was fully cooled again and I was eager to be back in on the action before it was all over. The assassins were scattering without even a message sent – but they weren't fast enough to get away from Claymores, and they each had two members of Blue Section double-teaming them.

"There's too many! It's a trap!" yelled one of the pirates – but they'd lost their Witch-capable ship, and they had nowhere to run either. The battle turned into a rout, and the rout into a massacre, with messages coming over the commset on all sides:

"You wouldn't kill me for a few credits, would you?"

"Please, let me go! I surrender!"

"You win today! Keep your cargo!"

But for today the Claymores were going to remain nothing more than a rumour, with no survivors to carry news away. We conducted a quick count as we watched the last criminals blow. All present and correct, and the *Quinquereme* undamaged.

* * *

For a live exercise, we thought it was an unqualified success.

Commander Voce certainly had something complimentary to say about it, addressing his thanks to "mysterious strangers who I have never heard of before" while turning back for his run down to the Coriolis station. We backed off to about twenty kilometres and formed a ring much like we had around the Witchpoint – close enough for all of us to keep *Quinquereme of Nineveh* in plain sight, but far enough away that only a few of us would register on anyone's scanners at a time until they got inconveniently close to the Boa.

We peeled off one by one when Voce reached the aegis, with no more pirates seeming to think it worthwhile today, and re-entered on the far side of the planet, closing formation as we did so. The Highlands and the Macrae estates lay forty kilometres below us as the thin air began to register on the Claymores' atmosphere planes. One by one we followed the Bull down in a wide spiral, touching down in succession on the field we'd left a couple of hours previously with eleven kills to report, no losses, and no enemy escaped.

"And Voce got the Python, ye say? That's no surprise – he's no' so very green at the game. Well, I'm thinking we'll keep this up for a week or two, and then we'll see if we can't root the knaves out of Ususor system altogether. Which'll not hold for good and all, but will make their profit and loss look the worse and cost them no small time and trouble to fix."

We'd been running the Claymores "clean" up to now, but they had hardpoints for missiles – which turned out to be unpleasantly draggy in atmosphere although, of course, they barely make a difference you can feel to a ship's performance in space. But Macrae got us all trained at both carrying and firing them in air. Parts of Ususor aren't habitable and don't belong to anyone, and these made good practice ranges for letting off rockets without hurting anyone.

"This'll be good practice for later," Macrae told us. "Extensive research has failed to turn up any pirate basing facilities on-planet – which is not to be wondered at; the noble houses would take a dim view of such goings-on – so ye'll not be missiling anywhere on Ususor itself. Later, though, you'll be having to go down onto some worlds and get your hands dirty."

The honeymoon period went on for another week or two. However Macrae was setting it up, he didn't reveal even to me, but I can think of any number of ways he could have managed it. He was plainly on first-name terms with a number of tough trader captains all over the sector – Voce among them although, as I was to learn, by no means the chief – and it couldn't be hard to include a coded message on, say, a tape of shrew cutlet recipes or zero-gee cricket highlights, which were being constantly couriered to all destinations. At any rate, we kept getting sent out on live exercises, we kept counter-ambushing, we disposed a number of assassins and pirates at no cost to ourselves, and all went well.

It was only a matter of time until someone slipped the net, though. *Lovat's Lament* was closing in to put the finishing touches to a Cobra I when a blue hole opened in the sky and the plasma-shedding villain disappeared. We had standing orders not to dive singly through any wormholes and we certainly weren't in a position to go through together, and all we could do was lock a Wormhole Analyzer on it and report back later.

Macrae was philosophical in bed that night – from which you can gather that our own personal honeymoon was by no means over, although the intensity had cooled to more bearable levels from the white heat we'd started out at. "That's the news out, then. It was going to happen sooner or later, and I never thought else. Well, but my backers are already sitting up and taking notice, and I've five more Claymores being commissioned, and my recruiters are due to report in any day."

"Does this affect our plans at all?" I said, co-opting Macrae's plans as a shared undertaking.

"No more than I was allowing for. We'll conduct that sweep I've been talking about and dispose of any basing facilities in this system; it'll take a little while to locate them, but thanks to Hugh's little box of tricks I've no manner of doubt that we'll find it. Energy signatures and communication codes, ye know."

I might have wanted to go over the plans in more detail, but Macrae had something more urgent on his mind, which meant that within about half a minute, so did I.

All of which meant that, shortly after Highlands dawn, all twenty of the Claymores were lifting off with a pair of missiles apiece, and our lobster genius's pirate detector pinging away. We were expecting it to be a long day, and we weren't disappointed.

A solar system takes a good deal of searching, even when you're looking for something that's likely to be the size of one of the larger asteroids – big enough to accommodate a Rock Hermit, or maybe bigger, even if smaller than a Coriolis station. We were expecting something that could store Quirium – maybe refine it, even – and missiles, not to mention hundreds of tons of cargo and some innocent-looking haulers to take it where it could be sold. Beyond that, we had no firm expectations.

Near the Witchpoint we turned up nothing but blanks, and the outer asteroids had nothing either. That meant a long foray sunwards, where a few chunks of rock were almost lost in the solar glare.

Then The Bull's calm voice: "I have a trace. Prepare to deploy."

*   *   *

It was a mighty big rock we were looking at.

At twenty kilometres we seemed to be seeing a slight twinkle, whether from metallic inclusions on the rock's surface or from artificial lights we couldn't yet tell. But Hugh Fitzroy-Badgerson's little gizmo was flashing it up as "Pirate Base" and that was conclusive enough for us. We fanned out by sections and locked sights on.

"Hold your fire. Missile launching," said The Bull. The temptation to plaster it with twenty missiles at once was obvious but the objections were equally so. We watched in silence as a single missile sped towards the rock, then exploded harmlessly many kilometres short. The alarm announced ECM and the rock was the apparent source. Inhabited for sure, then, and not one of the known habitations either.

"Inject to ten k's and fire missiles in slow succession. Make them ECM every single one separately. Blue section, laser it."

ECM is a valuable defence but it's not a cure-all; it takes energy to power it and that's not something you can spare much of when you have half a dozen laser beams boring through your shields. So the basic tactic is to make sure the enemy's ECM takes out only a single missile at a time, and he has to fire it up again for the next one... and we were packing a lot of missiles between them.

"*Loch Lomond*: Hostiles on the screen. That asteroid's launching."

"*The Rowan Tree*: Red section, take them."

I watched as the seven ships of Red section hared off after the new arrivals. We were still being held back as the reserve, with our own missiles unlaunched and our lasers cool. One by one the ships in Blue section sheered off, lasers overheated and missiling the asteroid one by one. It had to be feeling it by now although there is room for a lot of shield generation on a rock that size.

"*The Rowan Tree*: White section, laser the station." I had a lot of time for The Bull by now. He was fully committed to the ships he was chasing – the typical pirate mixture of small fighters and multi-role ships like Cobra I's and Moray Star Boats – but he was still keeping an eye on the battle as a whole. I locked on and let that rock have the lot, checked to see if there was a missile trace on the screen, then fired one. White section peeled off with hot lasers and let Blue section take over again. The amount of fire that thing was absorbing was...

"There she goes!"

...insupportable. Now it was time to mop up. There were excited yells coming from half the Claymores at the sight of the base blowing, but there were still a number of enemy ships scurrying about. It looked like a burst anthill, but ants can sting. The Bull bellowed at us to stop the chatter and get the comms board cleared, and everything went quiet for a moment while we got on with business.

"*Lovat's Lament*: I've got one on me!"

I looked to see where *Lovat's Lament* was in the confused whirl of red and yellow traces and the flicker of laser beams. One yellow trace was running fast and straight, a couple of reds after it.

"*Lovat's Lament*: I'm taking heavy fire from the Cobra III. Help!"

There it was. I settled my sights onto the Cobra III and set to work to strip away its rear shields. A touch of my injectors would put me right on its tail, but I was perfectly happy at the range I was. Someone took care of the Gecko that was also roughing up *Lament*.

"Stop shooting! I surrender!". That was the Cobra III – but we had our orders, and they didn't entail giving quarter, any more than pirates would if the roles were reversed. I gave the Cobra a final pulse and watched it blow.

"*Lovat's Lament*: Missile locked onto me!"

ECM jangled briefly, but the missile was still coming. The Bull called for any ship within range to ECM it again. Sometimes you get lucky that way. Sometimes you don't.

"*The Rowan Tree*: Inject, inject!"

"*Lovat's Lament*: Negative injectors!"

I swore, too softly for the commset to pick up. Nearly any ship will outrun a missile handily on injectors, but *Lament* must have damaged hers in the fight. I saw *Johnny Cope* fire a long laser burst from a shallow angle, hoping to score a direct hit on the missile. I heard The Bull call for *Lovat's Lament* to break hard... and then the missile blew.

I hoped for a long moment that *Johnny Cope* had scored a last-second hit or that *Lovat's Lament* had run the missile's motor down. But there was nothing but a cloud of dust and hot gas, which I found myself scanning uselessly for a living body that we couldn't have recovered even if it had been there.

"*The Rowan Tree*: Reform and return to base." There were no red traces left, and no wormholes. We'd succeeded one hundred percent with a single casualty.

On a low, slow pass over the loch, hours later, The Bull put us into finger-fours instead of columns by section. For those who don't know, read it from the left as follows: Two ahead of and above One, Three behind and below Two, and Four behind and below Three. But the final quartet was missing its Three; they call that the "Missing Man" formation.

Macrae formed us up by the loch just before sunset, all of us in ceremonial dress and a single piper playing, with aching appropriateness, "Lovat's Lament" as the sun dipped below the horizon. There was a fresh breeze blowing up the evening mist. At the last note of the Lament, Macrae himself lit a fiery beacon by the loch, and we stood in silence for two minutes.

* * *

At this point most hired escorts would traditionally have gone and got riotously drunk.

But it was different this time. At the close of the two minutes, there was a snarl of drums and half a dozen pipers struck up "The Black Bear" – I'd had the luck to draw myself a tune that, so the oldest sources claimed, used to be played to announce that duty was over for the day and all hands were to march off in whatever semblance of order they saw fit to go and entertain themselves until bedtime. We used it slightly differently, although it turns out to be a difficult tune to march to in step, following the pipes and drums back to barracks.

"Barracks" is not quite the word either for the Claymores' lodgings in the Highlands. I'd been exceptionally privileged on the grounds that I was sleeping with The Macrae, but there were guest quarters and to spare for the other flyers and the catering was hardly military mess standard either. It was likely to make us spoiled for spacer accommodation in future, as while it was short on high-tech amusements it was extremely long on old-fashioned comfort. Bear in mind that while I was young we were living on a world too primitive for soft sheets and electric heat; well, we were also far too poor for furs, and mostly had to economise on firewood as well.

The Macrae dined with us that night – and I say "us" advisedly as I definitely felt my place was with the other Claymores at that time no matter the pleasures of Macrae's own table. Once the initial shock of losing *Lovat's Lament* was over, everyone seemed to find themselves able to accept it easily enough. The Bull was quiet and thoughtful, but Macrae had a long chat with him, and as he said later on when we walked back down to the still-burning beacon, so far as he could tell the operation could not have been better run and led.

"I had high hopes of yon laddie from the first," he said, "for when it comes to battle competence, ye mostly needn't look further than the nearest Gelegeusian; they're bred to it early, though there's no' enough trouble for it to count on a planetary scale. No, the Bull's no' at fault for the one loss ye had – and, much though I grieve for young Emeraud d'Ivernage, I had resigned mysel' to losin' more."

"I wish we'd been able to pick him up though, the way I got picked up," I said.

Macrae chuckled softly. "Who wouldnae? But it cannot be done with what we have, Marilee. Even with the technology Neville and the Sassenachs have, ye'd need their level of practice and expertise. They are, make no bones about it, verra good at what they do, and we cannot match that unless we have the leisure time they have to learn it. Wi' anythin' less, I wouldn't fancy our chances o' pickin' up a half-dead cat. No. Be glad your own life got saved the once, lassie; we cannot count on that again, for you, me or anyone else."

He poured a fresh tot of whisky and held it up to the flame. "Forasmuch as it has pleased the Good Lord to take unto himself the spirit of our friend Emeraud d'Ivernage, we commit his component atoms to the quiet deeps of space, until the Big

Crunch or whatever else His wisdom shall ordain." And he poured a good ounce of priceless spirit on the ground and bowed his head.

"There's one thing, though," Macrae said as we started back to the house. "Your fellows are learnin' to mourn their dead with dignity. Till now, ye carried on like pigs, mostly. Whether the day went good or ill, ye had the one medicine; drink all your skin would hold an' shag all night wi' whoever ye could catch."

I chuckled at his coarseness, although the gentle pressure of his hand took the sting out of the crack about "pigs", and he went on, "Not that I'm about to cry out on all those who enjoy their dram, for as you know, I'm no' the soul o' temperance myself."

"And, for that matter, when it comes to the other thing..."

"Aye," he laughed, "which, to be honest, I thought myself done with for good and all. Well. Fighting men of any stamp generally dinnae live like monks. But there's measure in all things. We've seen off the friend we lost wi' some style, and no' the kind of desperation that's rooted in the fear we'll no' see another sunset ourselves. Tomorrow's another day, and we've fresh hands coming and new ships being delivered – and Clan Macrae will adopt them right warmly."

I had no doubt whatever about that. The new arrivals were ten in number and already dressed Macrae style, mostly human except a blue fat-cat from Xeesle who gave his name as "Tom" and, as far as I could tell, was born ready to discourage anyone who wanted to make something of it. But while Tom's girth was impressive for a feline, and he might have looked lazy to the casual eye, there was nothing wrong with his reflexes or his aim. He enjoyed skeet-shooting, except that unlike the rest of us he didn't use a shotgun but a pistol, and that with iron sights.

We had five new ships, and Macrae was going to spend some time to think about assignments for four of them, but Tom was an automatic choice for the fifth. Macrae told the other new arrivals not to be too disappointed, though: "After the work we've just done in this system, we have more funds being released to us, and the new ships are already on order."

While they were starting training, we were preparing to go out of the system: Maises, just under ten light-years away.

* * *

We had Macrae himself for company on this trip.

Since the Claymore is not Witch-capable, we needed a ship that was to get us from A to B. This wasn't out of the ordinary for most of us, who'd been flying one of the many escort fighters that are designed to just tag along with a freighter from system to system. Macrae was quite clear that this didn't make him the mission commander, though. Our brief was to help him safely to the station and then go off and look for trouble under The Bull's direction, then rendezvous for the return journey.

Maises is a multi-Jump trip from Ususor, of course, and Macrae took us to Veale first for a rest break. It caused quite a stir when twenty ships all docked together and twenty pilots all dressed in kilts disembarked. We mixed with the general traffic commanders rather than the escorts and kept ourselves to ourselves, but you can be sure that we were attracting attention.

"We're not going to remain a secret for ever," Macrae said at dinner. "People will see the new ships, and the strange dress, and when something odd starts in the systems we visit it will be but a matter of time before the chatter starts on GNN and the like. There's no help for it. If we could run to a Navy mother-ship wi' supplies for independent missions then maybe we could be more mysterious; but even the consortium I've been working on can't run to that, and even if it could, ships like that need resupply as well, and they don't get it at any common station either."

Veale station is staffed largely by the local Frogs, who didn't see us as any more exotic than the rest of the human traffic they get, and they were the soul of hospitality not least because Macrae was happily paying for the best service. We turned in at a respectable hour with the prospect of a short Jump the next day and a gentlemanly breakfast before we shipped out.

It's just about half a parsec from Veale to Maises, which is a hairsbreadth over two and a half hours in Witchspace. We already knew what to expect when we arrived; if there were any locals who might have been disposed to pick on an unwary trader, their enthusiasm was going to evaporate straight away when they saw a score of ships coming through together – which, by the way, calls for some precision flying to get everyone into the wormhole while it's open. Even Assassins have more sense of self-preservation than that; it's hard work to get victims rubbed out while making sure the law doesn't see you, and all that investment isn't to be undone by trying to complete a hit with the odds well against you.

"Intel had already placed the local facilities down on the planet," Macrae told us, "and I've had a drone go through the system to confirm. You'll find a globe of Maeses on your in-atmosphere HUD, and the place you're looking for is on a large island straddling the hundred and seventieth meridian south of the equator." Of course, meridians and equators are applicable concepts to all planets – once you know what the local prime meridian is, which is usually right under the Coriolis station unless the planet was colonised way back before the Coriolises became standard. North is defined by the sense of rotation of the planet around its sun; and either way, we didn't need to know what the definitions were given that the computer knew all that.

"Local industry's well up to providing some testing defences, so be on your guard. Here's the file." What you can get on the station is generally several rungs up from what you can buy locally – obviously, since even in the lowest-tech systems the station can refuel ships, and you can buy missiles in orbit even when the locals are running around in chainmail. Maises was plenty advanced enough for some sophisticated aircraft and simple missiles, but any hardheads would have had to be brought in from out of the system, as even Maises station couldn't manufacture them.

Of course, we could still have got zerg-rushed (whatever that means) if we'd been taking on the whole planet or even a nation state, but we weren't. What we had was a pirate base on whatever chunk of real estate the locals had never got around to developing for themselves – or which the pirates had stolen, with the locals too disorganised or outgunned to take it back – and that meant it only had whatever money the syndicate had managed to put into it.

We left Macrae behind at Maises station and headed for the far side. Whatever was happening would be well out of GalCop jurisdiction and, while it might have raised a stink on a planet with a one-world government, Maises didn't have enough organisation to even give backing to a strongly-worded letter.

"Stay alert," rumbled The Bull as we slipped into atmosphere. "There is no such thing as a milk run. Remember *Lovat's Lament*."

We fanned out, a dozen kilometres apart. It takes time to search a large island, even with a genuine Pirate Detector, but we were at high altitude and would be troublesome to spot from the ground, or to intercept.

Of course, the trouble with obsolete technology is that you forget how to deal with it.

After an hour or so we got a message relayed from ship to ship. "*Mhairi's Wedding*: I have a lock". The Bull called us all into formation by sections, and we prepared to go down.

We didn't see what was coming up until we got a whole bunch of white traces on our scanners. We naturally took them to be a volley of missiles, and some of them were, but some of them weren't. The reason's down to how scanners work.

*   *   *

I had to fill in the technical parts later.

Every now and then, when you are fighting someone in

space, they will figure they have only seconds to live and they will push the panic button on their escape pod. When that happens, the trace that was bright red (if you were fighting them) or yellow (if you were just a casual observer) fades to white. This happens because the escape pod release also shuts down their ship's drive instantly, leaving the ship drifting while the pod makes its escape – which, by the way, it also does while showing up as a white blip on your scanner.

The thing is, your scanner will colour-code anything with a drive system or a similar energy source. If it's a ship under power then it'll show as yellow, and if it's been flagged as a hostile it comes up red. Police show up as violet, and a few other objects such as fuel stations are coded for separately. But a generic non-planet-sized unpowered object comes up as white; and by "unpowered" that means "without a ship's drive". A missile motor's different, but the scanner's programmed to detect that too.

What our scanners weren't programmed for was a combustion engine. I barely even knew they existed; they were far too advanced for Qudira, and centuries behind the drives my Sidewinder had used and my Claymore was fitted with. No-one uses a combustion engine where a ship's drive will do... unless they can locally source combustion engines and fuel for them and want to save themselves an awful lot of credits building something that's never going to go into space.

Combustion engines are noisy, but they can still push an atmosphere ship along at quite a rate if you have fuel to spare. So what we had coming up from ground level towards us was a variety of ships and missiles powered that way, and our scanners were flagging all of them as "Alloys" - simple unpowered space junk fit only for scrap.

The part about being unpowered was exactly as untrue as the part about being space junk.

It turns out that a turbojet atmosphere plane can give a Claymore a much better contest in air than we'd expected. At eight kilometres altitude, and once we'd ECMed the swarm of ground-launched missiles, the jets could match us for speed, acceleration and turn, and their systems targeted us better than we could target them – mainly because every missile they launched showed up as yet another white trace, and we had too little signal to noise to be able to tell which was an enemy and which was a nuisance to be ECMed. Our computers couldn't tell when we were missile-locked, either.

The Bull snapped out a couple of concise orders and we started heading for the mesosphere. As the air thinned almost to nothing, we could start to make more use of our injectors, and the jets began to struggle especially in the turn. We could work with the air around us, but we were designed to manouevre in vacuum; they needed aerodynamic lift and air over their control surfaces. Fortunately, our shields had held off their missiles and the odd cannon-burst they'd managed to bring to bear, but *Lochanside* and I had both been given a good hiding by the time we managed to win clear.

At forty kilometres, it was another story entirely. We'd pulled the jets up to their ceiling and a number of them realized it and were making back for the thicker air below; four of them left the decision too late and found out that we had a line-of-sight weapon that wasn't being significantly attenuated at this height. (Whether the pilots we were up against were space-savvy enough to know what we were shooting at them with, or whether they were locals hired or coerced by the pirates, we weren't to learn. The Blue Mice that make up the bulk of Maises's indegenes don't go in for fighting like humans do.)

We circled at height, to see if we could lure more of them into coming up to the edge of space, but they were too wary for that. And we had an additional problem into the bargain:

"*Lochanside*: I'm reading a loss of cabin pressure."

Lasers and missiles alike don't tend to puncture a ship's hull on a minor scale. Whatever they'd been flinging at us had apparently managed a small penetration through *Lochanside's* shields. It wasn't killing damage for now, and the Claymore's shields would cover it through another fight – but it meant it wasn't airtight any more, and that's a serious matter for a spacecraft.

"*The Rowan Tree*: Understood. Any other damage, Claymores?"

He got a chorus of negatives, which left him to ponder for a few minutes. *Lochanside's* pilot, duAtha danAnn, was safe enough as long as we stayed in air – and we needed to descend to twenty kilometres to cut the rate of air loss to something safer – but he couldn't go to space unless we could get him something to breathe. We had a few choices: Fly to a safe zone where we could bring *Lochanside* down – and hope wherever we touched down didn't intern duAtha and confiscate his ship; find somewhere to land and make repairs or jury-rig something that would keep him breathing until we made it back to the station; or touch down briefly somewhere where we could take him off and either leave *Lochanside* for later recovery or blow it up.

Whichever we decided on, we still had a job to finish first. The Bull formed us up into sections staggered five kilometres apart in height and on the horizontal, and we headed down into the thicker air again. At least we knew what to expect. Sadly, so did the enemy. Any advantage of surprise we'd started with was largely gone by now. Well, we never expected it to be easy.

* * *

The Bull had had some thinking time, though.

"Red section, attack in line abreast. Choose your own targets but stay at ten kilometres minimum. Make a single pass and pull up to twenty kilometres, then reverse. White section and Blue section, follow in succession."

Something must have clicked in his brain. Lasers and ship's drives are as near inexhaustible as makes no difference, and even if we were aiming at a small enemy five kilometres distant, it didn't take much of a hit from our lasers to knock down one of these jets. A light beam's a straight-line weapon. They were having to try to hit us with projectiles which might or might not even carry the distance – and if they were coming up to ten thousand metres to try to engage at closer range then they were bringing the fight onto our territory, which favoured us more and more when we pulled up, and whichever section was following the one they were trying to attack had a clear shot at them in their turn.

They tried it a couple of times, and lost a couple of planes in doing it, and then we noticed there were fewer blips on our trace than before. As we later worked out, they'd had to start going down to refuel and rearm. That was our cue to go in after them.

We got a good visual on their base from five kilometres up, while we cheerfully ECMed any ground-to-air missile that was sent up after us. Local or imported, they had the standard vulnerable electronics, and some looked short on payload as well judging by the bang they made.

"*Loch Lomond*: Yellow trace below. Locked on. Type is Moray Star Boat."

"*The Rowan Tree*: Shoot him down! He's headed for the sea."

Loch Lomond and two other Claymores engaged and in moments the Moray Star Boat, *Captain Jack's Parrot*, was screaming for quarter. The Bull snapped out an order straight away: "Pirate, set down on dry land and power down. If you move one more metre towards the sea, we'll blow you. *Loch Lomond*, escort him down."

While *Loch Lomond* followed the *Parrot* to an inland site, the rest of us got on with plastering the base with everything we had. On a low pass it was possible to see the destruction in a good deal of detail. Orange flame fringed with heavy black smoke was rising from what we guessed must be a fuel depot for surface ships or the aircraft, and a level strip of concrete a couple of kilometres long was heavily cratered, which put paid to any ideas of launching further aircraft at us.

It may be hard to remember how to deal with obsolete technology, but once you've thought it through, you generally find out why the technology became obsolete.

An hour after we'd begun the assault on the ground base in earnest, there wasn't a vehicle moving or any sign of power generation. The Bull brought all the remaining Claymores over to where *Loch Lomond* was still circling the downed Moray Star Boat and sent "Pirate, exit your craft and stand one hundred metres clear. Wave some large object over your head."

Once the pirate had done as he was told, The Bull himself landed. That might not have been the strategic course of action but if Gelegeusians have a weakness it's a reluctance to avoid personal danger, and there was no way he was going to order one of us to secure the pirate and his ship while he himself stayed safely in his Claymore. We saw him approach the pirate, then head for the Moray, which a few moments signalled "Scots wha hae wi' Wallace bled. *Lochanside*, approach and land."

We took the poetry quotation as a sign that The Bull was in control of the situation, and so it proved. He and duAtha danAnn inspected the damage, but we had no repair facilities on hand. Still, there was very little left moving for hundreds of kilometres on either side, so The Bull decided on a compromise:

"*The Black Bear*, you now command White Section. Continue to orbit this location, radius two kilometres, as slow as you like. If *Lochanside* powers up, destroy it. If you are not relieved within twelve hours this time, destroy *Lochanside* and return to the Coriolis station. If you are attacked, use your own judgment but if you are forced to retreat, destroy *Lochanside* if you are able to do so without compromising your own safety."

With danAnn aboard the captured Moray Star Boat, and the pirate comprehensively in irons aboard her, Red and Blue sections headed back to space, which left us with a boring few hours in an extremely repetitive holding pattern with nothing to look at but cloud patterns. Still, that was better than some of the possible alternatives.

Night was falling when we saw a number of drive

flames heading our way, and a few moments later all of Red Section and the Moray Star Boat came into scanner range. The Star Boat was now reading as "Clean", too.

"*Captain Jack's Parrot*: Marilee, you're relieved. Well done. We've a pressure suit for young danAnn so we'll have that ship of ours back. Rendezvous at the station and don't start any fights."

That evening it was party time for sure, with the mission completed, everyone back safe and sound, and a captured ship and a prisoner into the bargain. Admittedly it was a civilized party, but Macrae was if anything even more prepared to push the boat out than usual.

"No. Yon miscreant's no' in the hands of the police. They're too accustomed to lettin' criminals pay their fines and go. The rehabilitation I have in mind involves a nice long chat wi' a few friends o' mine. We'll find out what he knows, and then... well, there's room enough on the Macrae estates where he can live a while."

* * *

No run of luck lasts for ever.

But sometimes it's not luck that's been managing your affairs, and for ever is too long a timescale to be planning for anyway. For most of us, long enough is good enough – and the "Claymore Scourge" lasted long enough to make a real difference, as Macrae intended.

On the back of those early successes came more backing and more recruitment. There is old money in the landed gentry on scores of worlds, and they don't like having their prerogatives trodden on, whether by random ne'er-do-wells and freebooters or by organised crime syndicates. The Claymores were few in number at the outset but they chose their targets well, where they had a tactical advantage and significant strategic gains to make. They achieved the goals of any elite strike force, which is to inflict serious losses on the enemy while taking few themselves, and while there would be losses to come, they would come after Macrae's initiative had gathered momentum and could absorb the losses.

It wasn't long before we had a second strike team, twenty Claymores strong, and then a third, and then a fourth, and while piracy throughout the sector was still looting trading convoys and lone ships, whole pirate enclaves were being swept out of existence. There wasn't a unified front that they could present – there isn't, so far as anyone has yet found, some mysterious "pirate island" where all the captains unite to debate, vote, and set policy. They're more like the disease that Hugh Fitzroy-Badgerson likened them to – a virulent infectious organism that can be highly successful at propagating itself, and that is perfectly capable of outpacing the immune system's attempts to stop it. But if that's so, we're like an antibiotic or even a nano-cure: directed, highly selective, and very able to outpace even the infection's rate of reproduction. And I was in it from the start.

That's something I pride myself on, but of course it was nothing more than a fortunate coincidence. If I hadn't fallen foul of a particular set of circumstances, I'd never have met Macrae. I had to lose a freighter, console myself with Terek, be run out on by him, meet and mistreat some anonymous bar-girl and end up thoroughly ashamed of myself, and run into a random kindly eccentric in a Coriolis station. When I look back, I honestly can't see a future in which I didn't die soon if I hadn't met Macrae. Instead – and in company with a number of hired escorts who seem to have been following a similar downward spiral – I found something that can only be called redemption. If that's not the right use for the word, then I never saw it.

Within the year, The Bull himself was off to Sector Two with a strike team and a senior member of Clan Macrae. The plan is to send another team through after a six-month wait, but it's difficult to check on progress until someone develops the mythical "Widdershins Drive" that would allow a ship to travel from Sector One to Sector Eight and so on back round the clock. But Hugh Fitzroy-Badgerson and his backroom lobsters were confident in their predictions for The Bull's future.

Longer term, we all have retirement plans. Macrae's adamant that none of us can be expected to fight pirates for ever and expect to live through it, and he's written a set tour of duty that means after a certain number of missions we'll be moved to the reserve list and training replacements. By that time we're looking like becoming a regular military – which, as I understand it, both the Navy and the police are tacitly approving of. Macrae observed to me that they were happier for the Claymores to be "inside the tent pissing out, instead of outside the tent pissing in."

But only to me. To the rest of the Claymores he's much more formal and never coarse – and to me he's the perfect Highland gentleman on almost all occasions. I can't describe how much it means to me that I'm the one person he can let the mask drop in front of every once in a long while, whether with a slightly rude figure of speech or a good swear at the state of the universe. There isn't, so far as I've ever seen, any force known to man, robot or alien that's capable of wringing a tear from Macrae, but I do believe that, with me, he's learned to relax enough to finally grieve, as have I.

Which implies something about our relationship; but we've no intention of formalising it. Turns out that it's entirely acceptable for a widowed Clan Chief to have a young lady about the place after a decent interval, and Young Macrae hardly needs a stepmother younger than he is. And in the likely event there's a Macrae Bastard on the scene in a few years, there's a place in Highlands society for one of those too – and over on cosmopolitan Gerete it would hardly even be noticed.

Macrae calls me all kinds of a fool to tie myself to an old has-been who'll be ready for a wheelchair while I'm still in the prime of life, for he's adamant about not turning to medicine to extend his life. "Lachlan deserves his turn as The Macrae in the way of nature, and there's more to a good life than the count of years," he says, and I know he won't be shaken on it. So I'll be his lover for a while, his nurse for a short time, and I'll have many years left to me to find another man who'll be half as good.

So for now I have good work to do, the tools and training to do it with, good companions and an adoptive family who couldn't be bettered anywhere in the Eight. I get paid more than enough for this job.

** End **

Afterword: From Elite to Oolite.

In the middle 1980s, the heyday of arcade games and the early years of home computer ownership, hobby shops did a lively trade in game programs that came on pre-recorded cassette tapes and, as a rule, took a good five minutes to load before the user could begin playing. The technology seems indescribably primitive a generation later. As I write, we have multi-core processors, memory by the gigabyte, storage by the terabyte, colour definition that almost matches the finest photography available, studio-quality sound, streaming video, and computers that talk wirelessly amongst themselves and by satellite and cable all around the world. Yet sometimes the programmers of the 1980s worked miracles with the tools at their disposal.

Miracle is an overused word; and yet, the writers of one game in particular transcended the limitations of small memory size, slow processors, tinny sound and indifferent graphics to produce a marvellously immersive game quite unlike any other. Children, teenagers and adults alike were drawn into spending many hours amid the thousands of planets and almost endless variety of a game that put them at the controls of their very own customisable spaceship and sent them out with a small cash stake to earn fortune and fame on a space trek with no end and no particular way to win other than to attain the coveted combat rating that gave the game its name: ELITE.

Within this world of vector graphics and, perhaps, a sixteen-colour palette, players could roam around trading commodities, add a whole variety of optional extras to their Cobra spaceship, fight pirates, earn bounties, even fall foul of the law; they could enjoy time and time again the thrill of dropping into a new star system, each one uniquely and idiosyncratically named, each with its own teeming population of humans or funny aliens with their documented peculiarities

165

ranging from a weird passion for food blenders to a penchant for edible arts graduates. Sometimes, jarringly, the computer would report something deadly serious instead, such as a persistent civil war or a planet-wide "evil disease". And sometimes there would be a special job to be done – a search for a stolen space fighter, perhaps, or a rescue mission for a handful of fortunate natives in a system where the sun was going nova. Then, when one galaxy began to pall, a flight to another was just one bolt-on extra away, and there would be a whole new map to explore and – who knew? – perhaps the rumoured multi-generation ship or giant space dredger.

All good things come to an end, and the hardy stalwarts of the home computer enthusiast in the mid-1980s – the BBC, the Commodore 64, the Amstrad CPC and many more besides – fell victim to obsolescence as the technological revolution continued. But many enthusiasts never lost their love for Elite, and in the course of time the opportunities afforded by the advance of technology lent themselves to a rewrite of the game using modern languages and the superior sound and vision alluded to in my opening paragraph.

Note well that word "rewrite". The initial objective was to recreate the gameplay of the original Elite – even down to the names of the individual star systems and their places in each of the galaxies. This was faithfully adhered to and the nostalgic games player can perfectly well recreate their 1980s adventuring on their modern computers. On the other hand, the availability of the new technology offered opportunities of its own, and it proved quite easy to make it possible for the players to write their own custom add-ons to the game. Thence came beautifully-rendered spaceships, the ability to haul contract cargo or deliver passengers, the option of having every ship you encountered given a name of its own, extra ships and facilities unique to one or another of the many government types established in the original Elite, and a still wider assemblage of optional extras to bolt onto your very own spaceship.

The revised game – now known as "Oolite" owing to

being written in an Object-Oriented language – is at the time of writing a dozen years old and still being maintained and improved. How many man-hours have been spent exploring the expanded Ooniverse, now perhaps featuring giant vacuum jellyfish, asteroid-mining bases, space casinos and planets with Saturnian ring-systems, would be hard to definitively assess. Much, without doubt, is owed to those enthusiasts who have built on so many extras designed to enhance the game-play of Oolite while still remaining true to the parent game. The packs of "optional extras" now number over five hundred.

One such extra in particular inspired the book you have just read. Oolite, provided you have downloaded the relevant expansion, allows the player to hire escort ships before embarking on a dangerous voyage. These escort ships will obligingly formate on their temporary commander's vessel and see to it that any evil-doers that seek to cause him distress shall have some distress of their own to take into consideration. I liked the idea when I first encountered it and it was only a matter of time before some highly natural thoughts crossed my mind: Where do these escorts come from? How do they get into the business? What must their life be like? And how does any honest trader even stay alive in a galaxy full of space pirates and worse?

Oolite being what it is, the natural way to address such questions is to write the answers for yourself. If my answers please the reader, though, I ask him or her to bear this in mind:

Without the tireless and unpaid work of the Oolite community, this book would not exist. They are due, at the very least, my heartfelt thanks and yours.

Douglas Porter
March 2016

Douglas Porter

ABOUT THE AUTHOR

As a small boy - and certainly up to the time I left primary
school in 1971, and to some extent after - I was a reluctant
writer although an avid reader. Indeed I fell foul of my
teachers in Changi Infants' School for both of these, the
latter as much as the former. I had a fondness for reading
everything in sight, even books that were many years too
old for me, and for many years could not see the point in
trying to write given the existence of so much that was
already written, all of it (to my under-eleven imagination)
far better than I could ever hope to match either for
content or for style.

This began gradually to change as I moved through my
teens and into my twenties, and there was a time when I
felt I did indeed have the proverbial "book in me" as early
as age 20. Still, that wasn't the way that my steps were bent
and I should have struggled to make a living on the
laboured prose that was the best I could manage back
then. Instead I joined the Civil Service and learned to
program computers for a living, and relegated such writing
as I was capable of most definitely to the realms of a
hobby or pastime.

From RAF child in Singapore to Bath schoolboy in the
1970s, to computer programmer through the 1980s and to
the turn of the century, and eventually to schoolteacher, I
gradually lost my reluctance to write while still retaining
my eagerness to read. It is truly rare for me to pick up a
book and not read it cover to cover, although I did manage
to make an exception for "Moby-Dick" while marvelling to
this day how Herman Melville was able to take a story
about a mad sea-captain's odyssey of revenge against the
monster that crippled him and make it boring. And
technology at length began to offer me an improved outlet

for my urge to write, since I found text many, many times easier to write by keyboard and screen than pen and paper.

Now in my mid-fifties, I have grown too slow and fat for outdoor sports more strenuous than a walk with the dog, but I still enjoy my music and the occasional appearance on the amateur stage -- not that I am in any danger of ascending to great heights in those pursuits, either. I am at least blessed with a supportive wife and sons, and the parish church puts up with my well-meaning efforts as their organist.

18710414R00101

Printed in Great Britain
by Amazon